The Nothing

by the same author

HANIF KUREISHI

The Nothing

FABER & FABER

First published in 2017
by Faber and Faber Limited
Bloomsbury House
74–77 Great Russell Street
London WC1B 3DA
First published in the USA in 2017

Typeset by Faber and Faber Limited
Printed in the UK by CPI Group (UK) Ltd, Croydon, CR0 4YY

A CIP record for this book
is available from the British Library

ISBN 978–0–571–33201–4

4 6 8 10 9 7 5 3

to Kier Kureishi

ONE

One night, when I am old, sick, right out of semen, and don't need things to get any worse, I hear the noises again.

I am sure they are making love in Zenab's bedroom, which is next to mine.

I wonder if I am imagining it. But I doubt it. These are not sounds I have heard in this flat before. We live in a large, open-plan lateral place. I never have the door closed in case I need to call for my Zee during the night.

I remain still and concentrate until I believe I am not delirious or enduring an LSD flashback. There are whispers, sighs and then cries. They sound like her.

It could be him too. My friend.

I have been expecting to die any day. The thought of death helps me to live and makes me curious. I can't see much and I am deafish in one ear, particularly in crowds and where I cannot see people's faces. But in the mornings, when Zee sleeps in, I lie back and listen. There is a world within this London mansion block. I hear the lift in the corridor outside, the steel doors rattling as they open and close, scraps of conversation in the hall, televisions, radios. Throughout the night I listen to foxes, drunks, police sirens, the distressed calling for relief, the secret life of walls and the buzz of my wife's vibrator, like a shaver.

In the morning I hear the birds. In a tree opposite this mansion block sit ten green parakeets, which Zee and I follow with interest. There is building work nearby. This area, Victoria, is constantly being renovated. I will not live to see its new look. I preferred the soot-black, more derelict London, which had some sublimity in its post-war despair. The mad were put in asylums, but the sane are worse off in their offices. This new world seems banal and exhausted. There's too much money in London. We've lived too long.

I was enjoying my decline and slipping away cheerfully. And now this happens.

The truth is always a surprise: my eyelids twitch with the effort of listening. My mouth is dry. My hips are ruined and my legs no good. With an effort, I turn my body a little towards the door, dragging myself across the mattress.

My arm stretches out for the light, and I knock my coffee cup to the floor. It makes a tremendous noise, like a saucepan struck with a hammer.

I am still.

Zee calls me a mistrustful husband, sceptical, dis-believing and keen to see the seamy side of things; desire and disease commingling. It is true that I imagine things for a living, and the imagination is the most dangerous place on earth.

But unless my neighbours have recently taken in pigs – which would be unlikely as they're Arabs – this new sound is a human one.

I hold my breath and stare into the dim light in the hallway. I can smell cigarette smoke. I think of how – even last week – Zee would comb my hair, stroke my beard or give me a coconut-oil massage. She would caress my chest and rub my ears. She'd remove my warm Uggs to fondle my legs and toe-toes as I reclined with a thermometer in my gob.

Unseen but not unheard, the noises don't diminish. I remain alert despite having taken my pill. Zee made sure I swallowed it. She was zealously kind earlier, surely a sign of unease, since she has been less warm recently. Eddie brought me the water, standing behind her in the door frame smiling with a mute complicity.

I said, 'Goodnight, Eddie. How will you get back to Soho? Or is it too late? Will you sleep on the sofa? You're welcome, of course.'

I eyed them. They were sure not to look at one another as I offered my kindness. It makes sense now.

Eddie nodded. 'Thanks, Waldo, that's kind of you, as always. I'll be comfortable on the sofa. See you in the morning. Sleep well, amigo.'

I sipped my double espresso, as I always do before I sleep. I love the taste of bitter black coffee in my mouth.

It was an ordinary evening. Now I believe I hear their voices, intertwined, light, cheerful as they lie together – naked, I presume.

After twenty years of marriage – and with a twenty-two-year age gap – I think this is the first time my devoted Zenab has been unfaithful to me. In fact, I am sure it is. I say: never believe what anyone tells you. But Zee is truthful. She would be appalled at the suggestion of dishonesty. Usually she is quite prim. Apart from one incident in her Indian childhood involving a murder, she was brought up respectably. She was too good for her own good, you might say. With not enough pleasures.

She has found some. She is making up for lost time. It is never too late. As the voices continue, I am horrified and excited. Sexual feeling might decline, but I have learned that the libido, like Elvis and jealousy, never dies. I know copulators of eighty-five. Who said you need an erection, a body or an orgasm for sex?

I begin to imagine what they are doing, the positions they adopt. Has she got onto her knees? Are they kissing as they resume their passion? One body, one beast.

4

I like to think I can see it. I was always a camera, having made more than twenty movies and documentaries. According to some film magazines, a couple of them stand in the top one hundred ever made. Or was it two hundred? I existed, as a film-maker, to see things. We directors are voyeurs working with exhibitionists. Now, at the end, I continue as an observer.

Looking keeps the world marvellous. And sex, even while I am immobile, indeed almost a vegetable in a wheelchair, can be intense. I recall the taste and smell of her, my last and only love Zee, the one whose body I enjoyed more than any other. I recall how shameless she became for me, and the games we played.

Now she is opening her mouth for him. Her fingers tug at his cock. Perhaps he is pulling her hair, as she likes it.

Working with sound and my imagination, I envisage the angles and cuts, making the only substantial films I can manage these days, mind movies. I brood constantly about the business of being an artist. I've managed several five-minute films recently, and they're not bad, freer than a lot of the stuff I did before, when I was nervous and there was money involved. I'll show them to my good pal Anita, next time she's round. She knows how to be both encouraging and damning.

Love changes people, they say. Or people fall in love

in order to change when they have been disappointed. Or when they are weary of themselves. Here something has altered forever. There will be revision. Who'd have thought it? Years of my life have become different in a moment.

I will need time to think this through. Time is at a premium for me. But at least I will have the rest of the night to consider it. I can sleep tomorrow.

In the morning I see there is no coat or hat in the hall. Or animal vapour. Eddie has scarpered.

As far as I'm aware, he has slept here at least ten times, folded on the couch. Often he is present when I wake up. He likes to stay for breakfast and discuss the news while dressing. He has a rabid appetite and a greasy mouth. He enjoys Zee's cooking, particularly her spicy masala omelette. He tucks in as if he hasn't eaten for a while and isn't sure where his next meal will come from.

I guess he saves money on lunch, before taking the bus into Soho. Sometimes he washes up and tidies a little before he leaves. In the past few months our flat has become his refuge, where he makes his phone calls, removing his shoes and putting his feet up on the sofa while repeatedly listening to the irritatingly uplifting jazz music he likes.

Now that things are progressing between them, he has made an early exit. He won't want to see me. Or, rather, have me see him. However, I know him well enough, and he has had a taste of the future. He will be back for another bite. I trust it will be soon.

Tonight.

I am keen to see how this new excitement will develop. He is playing with me. What a risk he is taking. I can be wild when aggravated. He has been overtaken by passion. He is not thinking. But I am. I am several moves ahead – at the moment.

TWO

The white face of the day.

Zee enters, throws open the curtains and helps me into my wheelchair. It has been three years since I walked and I still expect to be the man I once was. Impaired I might be, but I can tell you that old men can become more crazed as they age.

'Good night?'

She checks to see if I've pissed the bed.

'I'm not sure, my love. I was unconscious. I was gone.'

'What a mercy, Waldo. I like you unconscious at night.'

I swoon at the smell of her hair and body as she leans over me, giving me my morning kiss and caress. I like her to open her top and expose her breasts, slowly pull up her dress, or show me her feet while making agreeable female noises. This is how my eyes open to a new day. I prefer her toes to any sunrise. I even smile. She likes to see my eyes dance, my only organs with any gusto.

This morning she has showered and dressed already. She is efficient and even hums as she helps me into my chair.

I am keen to ask her what has made her so busy. 'Are you on a new vitamin?'

'How did you guess?'

With what is left of my low voice, I compliment her, telling her how fresh and vital she is looking and what an attractive woman she is. In her late fifties, witnessing my decline and suffering, she has been going to the pool, swinging weights, buying more new clothes than usual.

She is thin as a cigarette and has installed a running machine in my study, a room I rarely use now, but where my most valuable things are kept: diaries, notebooks, posters, storyboards, clapperboards, rare pornographic books, and a photograph of Zee's veiled mother, resembling a ghost from the Middle Ages. She helped me understand, when she and I sat down to talk about religion and charity, that I was a liberal and a dissident everywhere, even in my own bathroom.

There are birthday cards from Bowie and Iman, a photograph of me with Joe Strummer; another with Dennis Hopper when we were on the jury at Venice; and me in a dress and make-up with my Pakistani drag artists after I finished *The Queens of Karachi*. There are letters of praise and abuse from colleagues. And my masks. Once I donned the yellow one in the supermarket when Zee was pushing me – the jagged purple mouth causing consternation if not uproar in the aisles of Waitrose.

I like Zee panting beside me on her treadmill as I plan films I will never make. I wish, even in this state, that I had a final project, something to fill me with creative hope. Whoever heard of an artist retiring? We become more frantic to fulfil ourselves as we age.

While Zee studies her horoscope and prepares to go shopping, Maria the kind Brazilian maid comes to dress me.

After the exhaustion of breakfast, I settle down to look through the photographs and video I shot recently, wondering if there's anything I can do with them. Then I will make a voice diary. I like the world to know what I am doing. My head is always racing with ideas. I must let off steam before I boil. We artists are like capitalists, appropriating everything, stealing lives.

Before she leaves for South Kensington, Zee thanks me for my compliments.

'Will you go out for lunch?' I ask.

'Not today.'

'I hope we'll see Eddie this evening. He has some gulab jamun and new films for me. He knows I like to be surprised.'

'He will have something obscure.'

'I hope it's *Keyholes Are for Peeping*.'

I reach up to touch her face. She waits for my tremulous hand to make light contact with her skin. I wonder if she'll move away. She does, but not abruptly.

'It is pleasant for us to have company in the evening, Zee. Luckily Samreen and the kids will be arriving in a few weeks to provide some distraction for you. We must discuss her itinerary.' Zee seems to look at me but I wonder if she is absent. 'I worry that you get bored with my complaints and repetitions. Do you? Please answer me, Zee.'

'I wilted a few months ago when I fainted three times. Remember, you called me "pinched" and "bitter".'

'I apologise.'

'Oddly, I am content at the moment. Don't you notice me?'

'I see nothing but you, my Zeena. I want you to be happy.'

'You do? Thank you, Waldo. I will try to be.'

I search her face; she gives nothing away. If the djinn has returned after many years, secreting discontent if not euphoria, it is now concealed.

Eddie has been more than an acquaintance and less than a friend for over thirty years. We would have a drink or dinner together, or with pals, two or three times a year. He was good, roguish company, a scamp, ligger and freeloader, up for new adventures. I've long admired eccentricity, if not craziness – in others. He adores the famous, he's a dirty-minded raconteur, and I am a sucker for lubricious dick, cunt and arse stories. Anything involving secrets and weakness. Until recently, however, in the past five years I've seen him only intermittently. There are many like him in London, just hanging on, about to go under.

Eddie has always been evasive and sketchy, if not slippery when it comes to his affairs. I never quite believe anything he says. As far as I'm aware, he is still a movie journalist and goes to screenings and press conferences. I can talk about any movie and he'll usually have something interesting to say about it. If I want a comedy, which is often necessary, he'll have a good idea. I like to see a film a day, sometimes two.

Praise someone once and they are yours forever. Unfortunately, I think I flattered Eddie by mistake. I must have been in a positive phase. He began to visit regularly six months ago. He might be an idiot but he isn't stupid. He had turned himself into a self-avowed expert on my work and came to see us because of a planned retrospective and lecture at the NFT he was asked to organise. It was a good opportunity for both of us. I liked the idea of him doing my remembering for me.

So far there's no hard evidence that the retrospective will go ahead. Brilliant and incompetent, Eddie was

13

charged with the business of locating my early television films, material which was broadcast once and never seen again. I wanted him to find a film I made in the seventies about art schools and pop; another about dance marathons in the north of England, mods in South London; and some crude but lively pop videos from the early eighties. I'd be glad to have them available, but I am not that compelled by the idea. I have been admired plenty, and it is too late for there to be a permanent upswerve in my self-esteem. Dying I might be, but until last night I was reasonably cheerful and I have forsaken any need for the world to be my mirror. It's a relief to give up.

I try to follow my own thoughts but I have a scatty mind. This betrayal, this night thievery, this Eddie incident – if it is true, and so far I am not entirely convinced; who, after all, really wants to know what they know? – has awoken and concentrated me.

I must stay focused.

Today I sleep as much as I can in order to be awake later. I intend to follow up my investigations. If they enjoyed it last night, the chances are they'll enjoy it twice as much next time. Isn't the erotic an ever-increasing hunger which gets off on itself? As their pleasure multiplies they will be less discreet. Aren't we all looking forward to it? Suffering loses its horror if the victim can find a way to enjoy it.

It's a small world here. I don't leave the flat for days. We have a place in the country but rarely go there. One night, when I was still on sticks and heading for the garden to meditate, I fell over. I am heavy. And weighed down as I am with oysters, rich pies, summer pudding, goat's cheese and pistachios – slopping around in a lake of Bloody Marys, wine, brown ale and brandy – Zee couldn't get me up. We had to wait four hours for an ambulance. I think often of my death and how it will go. I wasn't keen to die on the floor, where it is difficult to speak. I expect my last words to go into the anthologies.

There is a buzz at the door. It is eight o'clock.

At last the exterminating angel comes. The night begins. Eddie arrives smiling, his arms full of packages: films, cheese, chocolate. An orchid for Zee.

'Give me a moment. Let me get changed,' says Zee.

Eddie and I watch football. I suspect he patronises me. He doesn't really like sport, which he thinks is for dolts. But it's difficult to be sure of anything with him. He wants to please.

My eyes are half-closed but after an hour I wake up to see Zee come slowly out of her room in her silk kurta pyjamas. Soon they are drinking cheerfully, as am I. Something is going on. He and Zee sit on opposite couches but they play with their phones like teenagers.

I adjust my fez and sip my wine, which I've placed on

a coaster on my zebra-skin stool. They are texting one another. I can see her smiling and tossing her head as she looks at her phone. She crosses and uncrosses her legs until her slipper falls from her foot, which pauses like a serpent in a forest. We both look at the eloquent foot. I suspect he wants to pick the slipper up.

Narcissism is our religion. The selfie stick is our cross, and we must carry it everywhere. Slowly I grasp mine and raise it.

I film the foot and other material. I am impatient, giddy almost with this descent into voluptuous maso-chism. Pain is such pleasure, and pleasure such pain. I am sure to be extra-quiet and feeble. Not that they notice.

I ask to be put to bed. I take a pill which I spit out clandestinely. It's ineffective anyway: you'd be better off giving an elephant an aspirin.

Eddie gets me into my room and helps to lift me onto the mattress.

The pillows hurt. He arranges them as I like them. His fingers are swift and soft as I mumble. 'Why is it when you see a cripple in a movie, you know he's going to be killed? Is it because he's already detritus?'

'I'll think about that,' he says, and turns off the light. 'It'll give me something to do later.'

Unusually, she doesn't come in and kiss me.

I lie there ready to listen. Tonight should be lethally

16

entertaining. My brain might be consumed by agonising flames, but I assume the loving couple have forgotten about me. I am becoming less important. They are under the lights, while I am fading. I'm a walk-on in my own movie.

Zee has always been devoted. She is the woman I always wanted. She gave up her country, her relatives, her husband for me. Once she said she'd love me even if I didn't have a penis. Did I believe that for a moment? Who doesn't love cock?

There's no life in her life, and she hasn't had sex for at least seven years. I cannot satisfy her in any way. She masturbated, I suspect, to romantic scenes in front of the TV. I hope it was Jane Austen. Perhaps Zee would love my tongue inside her. I can still waggle it a little. On a bad day just lifting my arm resembles Zeno's paradox. Motion impossible: an infinite number of movements which can never be completed. I can hold a drink, use my phone and turn my wheels, but I can barely do up the buttons on my pyjamas. What right do I have to be greedy or prohibitive?

I can't be a churl; I was young in the sixties. The seventies were even wilder and, probably, more corrupt. In those silly days when we were forbidden to forbid, when everything went and we believed orgasms were a cure-all, I had more than a good enough time, living in

17

a commune in California with the motorbike and live-in lesbians, sharing the love. Those magical fucks, when everything else falls away.

I had fuckability: a gorgeous man in flares and love beads, with wide shoulders, shoulder-length black hair and an ass you'd pay to bite. If you've once been attractive, desirable and charismatic, with a good body, you never forget it. Intelligence and effort can be no compensation for ugliness. Beauty is the only thing, it can't be bought, and the beautiful are the truly entitled. However you end up, you live your whole life as a member of an exclusive club. You never stop pitying the less blessed. Filth like Eddie.

I've learned that it is wise to beware of normality, and that virtue is a chimera. I've striven never to recognise common customs of fidelity or prisons of the conventional. Ethics are a pathological violence and the good an obstacle. I was, and hope to remain, a sensualist with a penchant for the Marquis de Sade as a moral guide. I will stick to this creed, despite the temptations of prohibition.

But I have also grasped that transgression affirms the very rules it intends to flout. Nothing supports the norm like deviation.

I want to say: it's only sex. And: never take it personally. Be tolerant; let others enjoy. Progress is the overcoming of taboos. Yet however you work at it, you can't take the meaning out of sex. Women still love more than men do. And it is not sex but love which bothers me. I am, I've realised at last, the sort of fool who wants to be loved exclusively.

It wasn't always that way. I misled myself: phoney ideals of masculinity – got from where, watching too many Westerns? – that made me think I had to screw all the women, even those I didn't want, reproaching my-self when I failed. The contempt for women who didn't want me. And the thought that all women were replace-able, that you could easily pick up another. And when I was unhappy, the idea that sex would save me.

I still have a 1960s sensibility. We took it for granted that the good things – equality, feminism, anti-racism, freedom for sexual minorities – would be extended. We believed we were enlightened. The good things would be good for everyone. But people didn't want them. We were elitists, that's all.

Now, ready to spring into inaction, with a little drib-ble on my beard, I lie down and pretend to be tired and even snore for their benefit. It's a good show. I worked as an actor for wild Dutch and German alternative the-atre troupes – often naked, sometimes on acid, peering through the celestial curtain – at the beginning of what others call my 'career'.

I hear something. Have they started? I settle down. I am receptive; all ears, as they say.

I think of my travels with her, the living creature I loved most. The food, wine, walks on Capri, in Paris and the Villa Borghese, Murree in Pakistan, afternoon sleeps beside her as she read. I contemplate her kindness, her caresses. I think of her fetching me a sweater when I am cold, and wiping my ass.

I am soon asleep.

Dead? No, worse: alive.

When I wake up it is to birdsong and blackness.

I stare into the darkness. There is silence; and silence is a strong sound. I groan and sigh. Even the lovers have given up. A night of non-knowledge and lumpish sleep. I sigh, and make the effort to turn over.

In the morning the birds trill, the lift rattles and Eddie has sloped off with my kippers, toast and coffee warming him. The world is back to normal. I closed my eyes and missed everything. It has gone. That night will never happen again.

'You seem annoyed and bad-tempered, Waldo. Is everything okay?'

'I had a bad night.'

'Let's hope tonight is better.'

It will be.

THREE

I connect my hearing aid. This is how seriously I am taking the matter. I am, as they say, going for it.

I inform Zee I want to listen to the wireless in bed. I often keep the radio on all night, the voices reassuring me I'm not the only person in the world.

Eddie swings by in the early evening, like a husband coming home from work. He is careful to offer me a little gift and show respect when he arrives. We watch the news together and he listens to my opinions and has the temerity to parrot them, particularly when they are peculiar. I wonder if he can feel my irritation and suspicion. If he does, he ignores it. The power is shifting here.

There is a flurry of activity as Zee gets changed. After drying her hair, a considerable and noisy procedure like a helicopter landing in your garden, she emerges from the bedroom wearing her pink – almost electric – dress, with pale tights and high shoes. She has a gay friend with a shop from whom she gets most of her clothes. She always dresses well and likes to be appreciated – the satisfaction of a woman who knows she's being looked at.

I set up the movie we have discussed. But she says, 'See you later, Waldo.'

'Yes, see you,' echoes Eddie. He fetches his coat. He wraps his scarf. 'We're going to have a bite. Won't be long.'

There you are. They are gone.

I scoot to the window, watching them walk up the street through my binoculars. Does she take his arm as they turn the corner?

If I were a dog, I'd bark and bark. I am left with the psychotic head of the television.

Making sense is always delusional, and I enjoy my magician's imagination, thinking through the scenario as I sit here shovelling mango kulfi into my cakehole. I play the parts and do the accents. I know the local restaurant they are eating at. Carlo, the Roman owner, is a friend. There is a photograph of me with Carlo in the entrance, between photos of him with Michael Winner and with Sean Connery.

'Where is the Maestro this evening, madame?'

'Waldo is poorly, I'm afraid, Carlo. He's declining. His thoughts are becoming increasingly unrealistic. He believes he's in Venice.'

'In the Danieli?'

I hear her bangles jangle as she touches her hair.

'Where else but having breakfast on the terrace? His

favourite place in the world. I can't bear to think of losing him. Please don't make me talk about it or I will
weep. Let me introduce Eddie, our dear friend. He is
very close to Waldo.'

'I am a documentary film-maker, curator, journalist
and collector,' says Eddie.

'Also a lecturer,' adds Zee.

'Good evening, sir. Welcome. A glass of prosecco?
Champagne? I'll send Pietro to let you know what our
specials are. I think you'll be surprised with the lasagne,
madame. I know you love almonds.'

'You always surprise me, Carlo.'

There it is, life is at a dinner table with a woman you
desire: blinding napkins, butter in ice, cutlery, melon,
sea bass and mashed potato, strawberry sorbet or summer pudding, double espresso – love.

If Pietro or Carlo sees them touching hands across
the table, I'd feel ashamed and murderous.

Too anxious to watch a movie or a match, I wheel myself to the other end of the living room. At the window
I drag the curtain aside and take up a position in the
eyrie of my caliphate. Pressing my bloodshot eyes into
the binoculars, I can see across the street. I sit here like a
fat fly at the windowpane, investigating fantastic lands
across the way. Despite the vastness of my solitude, it's
distracting up here watching people watch television

23

and children looking at screens. As always, sipping my yogurt lassi with vodka on the side, I record my mumbled and blurted thoughts into my phone. I enlarge my reality by speaking it.

From this palace of wisdom, I take photographs and I video strangers. I shoot sighs of bliss and featherbed clouds. Anything that looks unpromising.

I can't say life is any less interesting now I am almost paralysed and dead. The neighbours in the lighted cages of their apartments are compelling. Dinner parties are more riveting than wars, and are always an occasion for a close-up. But there's no sex. The sex is here, behind me, in every sense.

It is amazing how much people will let you see, and how little they appreciate the fact that they can come and go as they wish.

The couple eating supper in the apartment opposite appear frozen, their forks suspended in mid-air. I tap my watch; it must have exploded as my blood pressure increased. How much can Eddie and Zee eat? My wife and my friend are away a long time. Oral foreplay. They will be getting to know one another. Soon it will be happy hour. Preparing for a night of love, with the infinity of desire ahead of him, Eddie's penis will be twitching in anticipation.

I hope the food and wine are expensive. What do I

need money for now? It is irrelevant to me, and I want them to spend and enjoy it freely. Let everything go as you fall.

Hours later and the key in the door. They have returned.

Eddie watches the news while she is in her bedroom. I like a woman to take pleasure in herself. Zee is a Taurus and I believe that for Taureans the body is a church. She reveres – but also hates – her own body, as women tend to. Once she loved mine.

As she checks me I pretend to be half-asleep. She is in her dressing gown. I gasp: fresh perfume on her wrists and throat. I cannot resist: I raise my neck as she moves and catch a whisper of lingerie. Rapture: there are straps and rings.

I hold her red-feathered mules in the highest regard. I like a woman to look as though she just stepped on a budgie. I am that sort of man. But those shoes are not intended for me.

'I won't be long,' she calls to Eddie.

She won't be long.

Everyone is unknowable. I have to ask myself if I still love her. Of course I do. Love doesn't turn off like a tap when you want it to. The more difficult love is, the more it is love. Isn't that right? It is hard to acknowledge how much you need someone else. As soon as you do, you're

25

in trouble. This suspicion is making me feel a fool. The struggle for every man is not to look like an idiot.

With her it was the first time I wanted to be married to the person I was married to. We learned about one another. She liked me to sit on her face, even until she couldn't breathe; she loved to suck my cock for a long time. She shyly adored, for the first time, to have her rim and arse fingered as I enumerated her beauties in a low voice. To love sex, you have to embrace repulsion.

How banal, shocking and reassuring it is, then – when it comes to the oddness of existence – to wake up and find your lover has become a stranger who loves a stranger.

I need to get her back. I like her, and need a woman other men will envy. Even these days, a woman is the ultimate luxury item; a diamond, a Rolls-Royce, a Leonardo in your living room.

If my suspicions are correct, I will move like a serpent between the rocks. Watch me take that thief down. First I will smite him with madness, blindness and impotence, among other things.

Then I will urinate in his mouth and wipe my ass with his head.

FOUR

Eddie is one of those Soho characters you see at screenings, festival openings, parties and dinners. It flatters him to be included in all the hoopla, and he is first at the booze and hors d'oeuvres. Posh, well-mannered and attentive, he will try to charm you through the back of his head and flirt with his eyes shut. He was, I've been told, not bad-looking in his teens. A vulnerable boy in thick glasses with a rosy mouth and the arse of a cherub, eager to please. A magnet for paedophiles, it is rumoured.

He is usually sweaty with anxiety and smelling of drink, if not pubs, this overgrown schoolboy with his thinning hair, luminous scalp and cheap watch. Some disaster, involving his wallet, a train, a change of trousers and perhaps a woman – or two – has inevitably befallen him on his way to you. I dislike unsightly people when I don't pity them. They're always at a disadvantage when it comes to entitlement. If Eddie were good-looking, we wouldn't be having this trouble.

He has, however, made three documentaries, edited a couple of books, written for film magazines, taken part in conferences and taught somewhere or other. These I consider more serious offences. I think he may have sung in bars in a white jacket, also unforgivable. His French, they say, is immaculate, his voice smoky with public-school corruption and changing-room decadence.

Zee is happily drunk, with clouded eyes. But she brings my coffee, washes and changes me, and chats about Carlo, what was on the menu, who was there and how overdressed they were.

She is elsewhere. I can see it. Dadda, as she calls me, doesn't mind, I imagine her saying. She is preoccupied. She is beginning to fall in love. Everything seems new to her and the world is charged with meaning.

I lie down. I am still: going but not yet gone. I listen. I switch off the radio and tune in to another play. My hearing aid is an illumination. The world sounds un-usually loud. I can hear people dining in Paris, turning pages in Stockholm, making love in Rome and singing in Madrid.

Tonight, as I wait, I am a radio, with my receiver open.

I recall how Zee enjoyed discussing stories in the newspapers about older women who had taken younger lovers or 'toy boys' in Third World countries; desper-ate, poor men who'd deceive the women after marrying them. 'How could they be taken in?' she'd wonder. This will be something to bring up in good time.

The lights are dimmed. They play sweet music; I suspect they are dancing. Are they close together, pushing their fingers into one another's clothes? They cannot wait. Only temptation is divine.

It has started. Yes, I believe I can hear it all. I visualise the shape, colour and consistency of her body. I pretend his mouth is mine.

They move to the bedroom. I strain. But I can hear less. The scene goes on a long time, increasing in volume. I learn he is a horny little beast, fucking my wife. He might be cash-poor, but he's rich in jouissance, enviable at his age. Must be why women are suckers for him despite his looks and character. He's perfect: every woman wants a man to save.

You will be aware in my case of a man striving to be generous and understanding. I know that love is good for anyone. Eros the engine makes and remakes, reviving one's passion for living. I made her a widow the moment I married her.

I did say, 'When I am dead I hope you find a wealthy man with an attractive penis to look after you', while taking it for granted that when I died she would slash her wrists with a broken bottle, having first gone mad and ripped out her hair.

I know she will have a life after me and how could I be so cruel as to wish her more mourning than necessary?

Not that she didn't once moan, in the throes of love, 'You are the only man I ever wanted, the man who makes me feel complete.'

And didn't I know, when I met Zee and her husband while filming in Mumbai, that, after numerous wives, lovers, matches and mismatches, she was the end of all that searching. She was my destination: where I was always going. In my version of things, I had never been happy with any woman until I met her. She fulfilled me, becoming my mother, lover, sister and friend.

She worked on the film, cutting and sewing costumes. No one thought it a good idea for her to dump her decent spouse for a wild man who was beginning to bear an unfortunate resemblance to the older Elvis.

After the first month she cut my stringy hair herself and got me to wash every day. At night she monitored my money and turned out my pockets, throwing away my cocaine – which she'd never seen before – even as I swore I'd given it up. Whoever thought that pleasure makes you happy? Drugs had given me a faux bravery but they stopped me taking risks. Every outrage has to be earned; you cannot cheat reality.

I was either Stakhanov or Oblomov. I had become reclusive and ashamed, convinced others could see how I'd failed to make myself happy, despite everything I'd achieved. Hard-working and decadent, I'd been smashed, trashed, slashed, trolleyed and wasted. Like a lot of people, I needed to have sex every day – with whomever. I was too alive; I couldn't cope with my own energy.

Zee knew my truth and loved the smell and taste of me, the shape and curve of my body, my masculinity. She chased away dealers, women, whores, liggers and holders, the bums and strangers who stayed for weeks. She weathered my cold turkey and held my hand. She forbade me ice cream; I gave up Guinness for wine. Enjoyment is difficult. She made me less stupid: I learned to have pleasure without making myself crazy. She helped me recognise and protect my talent. An intelligent hedonist at last.

Work is always a diversion from the real thing, and I was in love. In the country we kept animals. We walked, lay in bed and had musical evenings, taking it in turns to play records. She likes show tunes and bossa nova, but came to appreciate Curtis Mayfield. We danced together.

I feared that contentment would ruin me as an artist. I would lose my edge, fury, aggression and bitterness. I'd have better things to do than entertain the public. I'd seen it in others. But being with Zee was an experiment I had to make. I'd been over-defended. It had kept me from deeper, more disturbing and exciting experiences. I wanted to see, at last, how close I could get to a woman. How close I could get to another human, while we remained separate human beings. I wanted to lose myself and become utterly dependent. I wanted her to change me.

Another thing. It was curious: from the start Zee told me not to spend the night beside her. Did she find me unattractive? Did I snore, sweat or curse more than usual?

She had a djinn. An aunt had used black magic on her.

As a fan of the occult, I insisted on witnessing the djinn's business. These really were the black hours. I've never known anyone suffer from such nightmares. She'd scream, and often kick and punch me. She'd cry out that she was dying. Being murdered, more like. I never left her side. She was comforted and less ashamed. I have never abhorred a single thing about her, and I always tell her that.

Zee and I married, to show our seriousness. I wanted to be a husband, but had to become a stepfather too. I took care of her twin daughters, who could be a handful and sided with their meek father. They were brought up to be respectful but I had kidnapped their mother, willingly, and them, unwillingly. I learned the hard way what a catastrophe being a step-parent can be: how much hate and humiliation you are obliged to swallow. These children, who were not mine, but belonged to a decent man, were more difficult than any movie I'd made. Some days their cruelty was unbearable. We sent them to their father when we could. I went into therapy when I found myself wishing they were not there at all. I believed I was even prepared to give up their mother when the kids made me into an ogre I couldn't bear to be.

I took good advice, and survived. The achievement of loving a woman meant more to me than anything else.

At last we settled the kids in American universities, for which I paid. I got one girl through rehab and madness. Now they are doing well. Jasmine works in hotels. Samreen reminded me of myself: an indolent, grubby and vile-tongued teenager, who rejected most education, became a vegan and a slut, and disappeared herself from several expensive schools. I rescued her from police stations twice. We almost lost her. In her late twenties she gained momentum with a sudden ambition to become a doctor. She sat down and studied. She became a dedicated gynaecologist, working with poor women in Los Angeles. We have come to like one another. Both girls have taken my name and they can make me laugh. I am proud to be head of this family.

In the last ten years I declined and became weak. Cocaine had done for my heart. I have a stent. I also have most illnesses: diabetes, prostate cancer, an ulcer, early MS, constipation, diarrhoea and only one good hip, a

cough, phobias, addictions, obsessions and hypochon-
dria. Otherwise I'm in great shape. Zee takes care of me.
It is her responsibility, and love.

Until now: there is much muffled talk and laughter
until at last near-silence.

He is melting her down. Soon they will be doing
things for the first time, sharing confidences, songs and
kisses, exchanging jewellery, discovering one another's
likes and dislikes, becoming a couple, an essential part of
one another.

I can catch some of it but not enough. I will need a
better way than this to receive the minutiae.

Then, if this betrayal is real, you can count on me: I
will do something stupid.

FIVE

I still wake up as a young man, until I begin to move. However, I decide to decide. There will be motion. Something must happen. I will not surrender. We should go out. It might change something.

I dislike the country; I despise the suburbs; the city is a trial. I inhabit a small world. It's no loss. Recently Zee and I went on an enjoyable day trip to West Kensington: the Talgarth Road was our Route 66. We've discussed sampling the ecstasies of Acton, a place as exotic to me as Liberia. Graham Greene would have had a ball.

In the next few weeks we have two social events lined up, followed by foreign trips. Zee and I discuss them. We will attend. It is too enclosed in here. We need more life.

Growing old isn't for pussies. Despite my disabilities, Zee and I still carouse. It's an effort; I do it for her, since her pleasure is mine. She loves parties and openings. Being a little naive, she considers them glamorous and goes keenly through the invitations which still arrive every day. She replies, organises a car to get us there, and checks out the facilities at the other end. The nurse will wash and dress me, and in I roll in my chariot of ire. Old friends come and take my hand, crouching down next to me to hear my bad news and give me theirs.

At lunch she puts a 'stiffie' – a stiff envelope – to one side.

'This would have been an opportunity.'

'We must go. Zee, I've been so inactive—'

She says, 'Last month there were three funerals of your close friends and two memorial services. And one deathbed scene.'

'I've neglected you. The dying are egotists. Let's do it—'

'I think Eddie should help us,' she says.

'Eddie Warburten?'

'He's kinder than you realise.'

'In what way?'

'He squeezed that spot on the back of your neck which I couldn't bear to touch, and gave up two days to take you to the doctor's and to hospital. He's better than any assistant and never complains. He helped you in the shower.'

She's right. It's not often a film critic fondles your balls. I was naked, splayed on a stool, as he rubbed my ruined body down with a flannel. I pity him having to touch me, but he wasn't afraid. I'm too intelligent for shame, but he gave me no reason to be embarrassed.

He dressed me and got me into bed: strenuous work.

'Eddie has a knack with bow ties. You can't wear that torn Frank Zappa T-shirt all the time. Those stained shorts are for the bin. The balaclava makes the neighbours think you're a terrorist. You know I love your silver hair, Waldo. You should show it off.

'Anyhow, you enjoy his company: I hear you laughing, or, rather, coughing up your lungs with that ganja he gets for you. It was you who invited him here – not me. You encourage him with his projects, and asked him to stay the night.'

Even I tire of myself. It is essential for her to have some relief from me.

I say, 'Let's consider this. Most of my friends and allies are dead, and many of my friends disappeared once I stopped being a working artist and could be no use to them. But why not take Anita, if she's free? They'd rip the clothes from her back.'

'Would anyone look at me? I'd feel undermined. Don't you see enough of her? How often does she call?'

Zee decides to take Eddie shopping. He'll be fine once he's been redecorated, or 'sharpened up'.

'Like a knife?'

It is serious work. The rebranding of this mildewed ear takes several afternoons. There is, I admit, much to do.

They have been buzzing around London in taxis.

Eddie is prepared at last. We open a bottle. He shows us a nice suit which fits him, unlike most of his clothes. We witness a new raincoat, several jackets and a leather bag slung across his puny chest. I stare at his hair, which my Macedonian has cut. It shines like a bird's wing: jet-black, for the first and, I hope, last time.

I notice, when eventually I look down – and this is a stomach-emptying fright – that he is wearing my crocodile-skin Italian loafers. Even the crocodile would blush.

'Good, eh?'

Zee is proud of him, this comical new man with new teeth, looking slightly sheepish, if not embarrassed. A flute-playing kid with a music certificate, patted on the head by his mother.

'Eddie, aren't those my shoes?'

Zee says, 'You'll never wear them again and they fit him like a glove, Waldo. They were on their way to the charity shop with everything else you'll never need again.'

Eddie adds, 'Waste not, want not. We saved money there.'

I'd be shocked if I weren't paying for the toad's renovation. There is nothing to indicate he has made a contribution. Or that he has any independence. I am puzzled that he will allow himself to be patronised in this way. Where is his pride?

He is in a jaunty mood as he inspects himself in the mirror from various angles. He attempts to distract me with slanderous stories about movies, directors and actors.

Zee has bought herself an Algerian shawl and some pretty dresses to 'cheer herself up', along with some furniture and rugs. I have to admit, the place looks less blighted. We have neglected it. Many of the drawers are broken; the fridge doesn't shut properly; the bathroom has become a danger. I try never to lower my eyes, since the carpet is stained, and there could be dead animals down there.

Now Zee and Eddie are reborn, we launch ourselves into dinners, galas and parties. Without anything being said, he accompanies us.

'Just in case', as she puts it.

When you're in a wheelchair, people literally look down on you. Eddie is useful when we are out, forever behind me, pushing, smiling, keeping fools away where necessary. He recognises faces, and knows how to whisper a few words in my ear as an old friend approaches and their name and accomplishments escape me.

We fly to Spain for a couple of days, where, crazy with the heat in my orange kaftan and flippityfloppity hat, I'm showered in clichés and receive a life-time achievement award, always an anticlimax, and apparently signalling my benignity. Zee pushes me out on stage and I smile, wave and weep while she thanks everyone on my behalf. I despise such respectability, even at my age.

A few days later there is what I can only describe as the big one. My final lap of honour. We go to Cannes. Once, as chairman of the jury, I was given my own car, a driver and two outriders with flashing lights. I strode through crowds and photographers like an emperor.

As I am rolled towards the stage through the pouty-mouths, playboys and Euro-stardust, I receive a standing ovation. Eddie helps – there really is much pushing, pulling and carrying – and he walks behind us at all times. While he is with me, no one can snub him, ignore him, or refuse to take his calls. They must take his hand, sit next to him at lunch, hear extended accounts of his projects and be offered the opportunity to invest in them. He is in the photographs, passing me a handkerchief to weep into. I weep as easily as others ejaculate. It makes a good impression.

After the unnecessary fuss over me, the couple park me in the hotel with some bad movies before rushing out to parties with my invitations. I hear that Eddie was greeted at one as if he were me! They gossip, dance and revel until their feet disintegrate, strolling along the edge of the sea to cool their burning soles.

She returns to our suite at the Carlton early in the morning. I'm half-asleep but say, 'Where were you?'

'Sorry I'm late, darling. I heard something. Gossip. It took a long time. Of course, I will never tell you. You don't deserve to hear it. Not this time.'

'You know you will tell me, baby. But, all the same, I love you to tease me.'

When we return to London I take a long lucubration and make my voice diary. I am becoming more determined. Eddie is taking too much for granted. I will have it out with him and begin my jihad. My wife – and now my hospitality. The world has tilted a little. Everything in it is going wrong.

All my working life I've dealt with producers, publicists, stars and fools. Some I've got through to and others I've had to smack. A few were wrestled to the floor in the long term.

He and I will talk. I will wait until she's out shopping and he is here on his own. I will have him on toast.

One afternoon the moment arrives. I am in my chair watching him organise the DVDs, my pathetic fists clenched. I know I must act.

It is amazing how he gets on with things without

41

paying me any attention, as if he hasn't lapped her sweet snail right under my nose while wearing my shoes. He even whistles – I can see his lips twitching – which I consider a sure sign of wrongness. Perversion has its limits for us normals, unfortunately. It has taken me a lifetime to become as uninhibited as I am. I still wish I could be more committed to the weird.

'So, Eddie . . .' His every movement has become a flagellation for me. He turns. 'Tell me something—'

'Yes? Sorry, Waldo, can I get you a drink? Do you know where your glasses are?'

'No idea.'

'Round your neck, dear friend. Do you need the toilet?'

'No. But you might.'

If he has a mind, it is elsewhere. I ask him to put on 'Helter Skelter' and insist we listen to it twice through my sixties speakers. My blood heats. I'm pumped until I believe my greatest regret is not doing more harm.

'Anita's favourite song,' I explain.

'Is she coming here?'

'Would you like to meet her? I could arrange it.'

'Please, you know I would swoon, Waldo. But you've always kept me from her. You tease me, sir.'

I say, 'Eddie, you're here – in my flat – a lot of the time, but I don't know you any more. It's been a while since we talked. Are you married at the moment?'

'Not exactly right now.'

'You have a lover?'

He says, 'I have been drowning. Waldo, things have become difficult for me, man. It's a hustle out there. You're well known and admired as a master. Lower down it's constant graft to get a few hundred pounds here and there. If you're lucky . . .'

'Remind me how many children you have.'

'It slips my mind too. Five. Two of them are still at school, and one is at university. One is disabled. She won't grow. She needs constant care. It's a misery and has unnerved me for life.'

'I'm sorry.'

'You might remember, there are three mothers, and they pursue me for maintenance, school fees and more, which I can't cover.'

'Isn't it your duty, Eddie? We all must struggle to remain upright. You see it in me, the daily work of decency.'

'It's unmissable in you, Maestro. You know I have several schemes in the air. But I can't become a millionaire overnight. Still . . .'

He looks jittery.

He leans towards me. As a favour and education he talks about the new Baal: precariousness, the lack of work, of social support and pensions. That we have created a world of billionaires and paupers. He informs me that money is the devil, and that the financial class uses debt to control the population. The cannibalism of capitalism, the emptiness of democracy and hyper-neo-liberal alienation, commodification and stupidity; the virus of money and the way the poor bust their balls to save the financial class – he lays it out for my benefit.

'I have a vision of your future,' I interrupt. 'Transgression is the new norm, and enterprise the new word for cheating others. Politicians, entertainers, lawyers – the most respectable fill the prisons. Eddie, can I suggest you go into crime yourself, albeit disorganised crime? How can you afford not to?'

'Very funny, Waldo. No wonder the Queen was keen to pin that CBE on your breast. I'm surprised you weren't offered a knighthood. Do your best work at a young age, and join the ruling class, eh?'

He goes on: 'You, your friends and contemporaries are the most talented people around. But it would be foolish to think that the whole world is like you. Weren't you a Leftist? A Maoist? Didn't you stand outside the factory gates at five in the morning selling revolutionary newspapers with the activist actors?'

I raise a finger to pause him. 'Eddie, never think of me as anything but a man of the people with a taste for exclusivity. A snob with a common touch. I've asked

Zee to toss what's left of my body into a pauper's grave wearing diamonds. Where do you actually live?'

'I'm still in a small shabby room with a single bed in Soho. The bathroom down the hall with a broken window. The landlord a savage who walks in whenever he likes and takes what he fancies. Luckily a friend is helping me find a better place. If I had a grand for a deposit I'd be set.'

Human beings are double or triple. But one thing I do know, as any *noir* would instruct, is that they want money more than anything else. They are, in that regard, totally reliable.

I say, 'You tempt me, Eddie.'

'I'll be gone.'

'I want you to be settled. I'd worry otherwise.'

He looks at me. 'What are you saying? You'd get the money back.'

'Don't patronise me.'

'I'd never dare, sir.'

I say, 'Ask Zee for a grand. Like the Queen, I never carry money. And don't forget, Eddie, if there's something you need to say, you can come to me. I am a big ear.'

When Zee returns he hurries across to her with some enthusiasm. They go across to the kitchen. It is not long before I see her hand over the cash.

45

Yet I cannot stop laughing. I intended to dissect Eddie and feed him to the squealing pigs down the hall. But I ended up loaning the bamboozler the bread. Milton refers, in *Paradise Lost*, to a 'devilish engine'. Eddie is that motor, roaring in my living room.

I know laughter is not good for me. I could shit myself or have a stroke. How vulnerable I turn out to be; how Eddie tangled up this wily old fox by appealing to his conscience! Despite my efforts at a Nietzschean elevation, the cunt melted me like an ice cream under a blowtorch.

I may be a sucker – you will recognise that I have more than enough foolishness in my nature – but momentarily I have bought happiness. This jester has cheered them both up.

Zee looks delighted, as Eddie slips the wad in his pocket, grinning – but not too much – at my absurd generosity.

She believes I have seen sense at last. Everything is going as she wishes it to.

Then an odd thing happens.

SIX

Guess what? He has the money and he disappears. A day passes, then another, and another. She waits; even I wait. She stares at the door and at her phone. She paces; picks things up, looks at them, and puts them down again. Still the shit doesn't show up.

The manic intoxication of love forces her out. Like God, I am all-seeing. In other words, I follow her moves on my phone. She comes home wet and exhausted, having looked for him in places I'm sure she's never been: pubs, clubs and dives in Soho, the offices of movie magazines.

I wake up expecting to be loved and then I remember that I am not.

She doesn't come to me in the morning, let alone give me a kiss. She has panic attacks, sleeplessness, 'vice-like' heart pains and requires an ECG. She could easily die before me; she'd often thought she would. With a migraine of sledgehammer-and-suicide intensity, she takes to her bed and pukes and mewls. I manage to fetch her a basin and hold it for her, my weak arms trembling as

I observe her dark hair, kissing it when I can. Since her loneliness and anxiety chill me, I sit beside her, dozing.

It isn't until I begin to relax that I have some idea of what a strain it can be living with a stranger who sucks on your wife's nipples, biting around that pretty ring, the areolas.

'Has he gone for good?'

'I don't know.'

I say, 'Darling, it is just us for the first time in ages. If my legs worked, I'd stretch them. If my arms did, I'd rip off my shirt and smack my chest. Won't you do me a favour? Just a sniff, baby. Will you show me yourself?'

From a Muslim heritage of modesty, if not severity, under my tutelage she became sexual. She'd been fondled by her stepfather and an uncle. She'd never had an orgasm, even in masturbation. Her husband never touched her cunt, never sucked her or offered his cock to admire. She attempted to reduce her sexuality to banality and even ridiculousness, as some people succeed in doing. 'Why does it matter?' she said. 'Most people have little or no sex. Or even love. Can't we forget the whole thing.'

The humiliation of desire. We smoked weed together and did stuff we'd never done. Sex is like art: if you know what you're doing, you don't know what you're doing. It took us a year to create together the sex that sent us. At last we found love and passion in the same place – in love's Holy Grail, one another.

Sometimes, as I rest, she will lie down next to me naked, allowing me to look at her. Now, reclining in my favourite chair, I decide to see what she will give me.

She is usually willing to pull her panties down and open her legs, to show me her pink lips. She isn't averse to masturbating, a show which always elevates my mood. She might raise her stockinged foot to my mouth and let me suck on it while I paw at my dick.

She likes to be looked at and appreciated. She swims most days, doing seventy lengths in the morning. Her ass is still firm. When I could rim her little hole, or halo, as I call it, and push inside, she'd almost slice the tip of my tongue off.

'Not right now, Waldo.'

'Please, kiss me on the forehead.'

She shakes her head. 'Like you, I haven't been well.'

'I repel you. Can't we talk?'

'What is this about, Waldo?'

Her eyes are red.

'Are you sure Eddie's good for you?'

'What do you mean? You don't want someone to talk to me? To listen to me? To take me places? You're becoming more of a rude man than you were before,' she says. 'You want me to be alone. You're old, very old, Waldo, and I want to have a life. Can't you admit you were harsh with him?'

'Was I?'

'You have savage eyes. You interrogated him. You looked at him the way you used to look at the actors. Some of them hated you—'

'I was responsible for some of the best work those turds did. A slap across the chops can only benefit a glove puppet. You know what kind of man Eddie is.'

'According to you, what sort?'

'I imagine he's fled with a woman to a Brighton hotel on her husband's money. He's never earned a living.'

'How would you know what a living was, sitting in a chair all day wearing an old tie-dyed T-shirt and staring into people's homes through binoculars?'

'I'm aware of his reputation.'

'What reputation?'

'As a chancer. A man we used to refer to as "a shit". Someone who gets to a restaurant early to order drinks on the other's tab. Someone who would extract the milk out of your tea, as my mother would say.'

'That's unkind.'

'We're not composing an article for the *Encyclopaedia Britannica*. That is the way of gossip. When we fucked and came, we liked to talk. Why suddenly so prudish?'

'You mock and bully him. You make him find things you need and berate him if he can't.'

'He's an upper-middle-class, public-school-educated, middle-aged white man. His parents lashed the natives overseas while promoting Western values. He's had more opportunities than anyone on the planet. So he's a fool.'

She says, 'An outrageous thing happened which stunted and eventually ruined him—'

She stops.

I say, 'You've lost the ability to talk intimately to me, Zee. I'm afraid Anita might become closer.'

'Please, don't try that. Remind me to go out next time she's here telling us which famous director or actor tried to seduce her.' She says, 'Do you have any idea what went on at that famous school of Eddie's?'

'Ah. So it is true. Is it? Once you've informed me, I will reflect on it.'

'He's told no one but me and a friend. You'd take advantage. You know you would.'

'You've never held back, Zee. You said I could make you do or say anything. And you know I can close down our bank accounts.'

'You'd starve me, would you, pig? I know you wouldn't dare.'

I extend my tongue, like a lizard expecting a fly. 'Spill the beans or apply a flannel to my forehead.'

'You are corrupt.'

'Don't you love that about me?'

'I don't know what I love about you any more.' She sits opposite me, and she isn't laughing. 'Waldo, you know very well how the British disposed of their children – far out of sight. The school was cold and far away, in the north of England. His parents, like characters out of Somerset Maugham, were sipping gin and tonics in Hong Kong.

'Eddie worshipped his English teacher, Bow; handsome, charismatic, anarchic – so Eddie said. A man he was determined to please. You know how he is . . .

'As you say, Eddie was the future of England's ruling elite. He was thirteen, and terrified all the time. There were spankings during the day for minor infringements. The real stuff was at night.

'Eddie was clever and pretty but awkward and hopeless at sport. One day Bow pointed at him. He had been chosen to go to Bow's study.

'He looked forward to it from the moment he got up, counting the minutes. He'd prayed to be picked, after smiling at Bow, the teacher who was considered a "connoisseur", who seemed free and unlike the others. Eddie raced through the freezing corridors in his damp overcoat. He wasn't ignored or neglected now.

'Bow announced he would give Eddie a special name.

He did this to his favourites. Eddie nearly burst with pride. He was called Dear Pussy.'

'Dear Pussy.'

'Don't ever say it to him. Don't smirk.

'Bow lit the room with candles in wine bottles. It was decorated with rugs, books, reproductions of Expressionist paintings, and all that. And a life mask of Keats, can you imagine?'

I close my eyes. 'You're doing well. I'm receiving it in 3D.'

'Bow would open a bottle of wine, offer Eddie a Balkan Sobranie and play him his favourite records: the soundtrack to *Lift to the Scaffold*, I think it was. You'd know it. And Dizzy—'

'Dizzy Gillespie.'

'And Nina Simone. Eddie was bowled over by this elegant dandy, still wearing his sixties cravat, Chelsea boots and hippie hair. Bow gave Eddie *Dorian Gray* and hugged and kissed him. Eddie was compliant. You see, he had gone there cheerfully. Eventually, well – he sucked him off. He'd never done that before. God forgive me, but provide me with the strength to say it—'

'Please.'

'He was made to strip and offer his bottom. The man made it easier with margarine. Waldo, you've got the filthiest mind of anyone I've met. I won't describe any more of the rape. It was painful, needless to say. Despite retching at the smell of semen – and having to visit the matron, who said nothing but applied iodine – Eddie was keen to do everything Bow wanted. The next day he returned. The next, too. It went on for a long time. Bow had a dressing-up box. Eddie loved to pose for him as Peter Pan.

'But Bow preferred Eddie as Liza Minnelli in *Cabaret*. He bought the boy high heels, a wig, eyelashes and lingerie. He liked him to sing "Tomorrow Belongs to Me" in his cute voice. Eddie was gazed at by Bow with such admiration and desire he felt more wanted than ever before in his life.

'Bow took Eddie to the cricket at Lord's. There were tender study trips to Florence and Venice. For the first time the other boys looked up to Eddie. Bow often had his arm round him. The Godfather protected him. Now and again, however, other boys were invited to be Bow's intimate intimates and even to wear the clothes, to pose and be photographed.

'Little Eddie wept. He was jealous. He wanted to be loved exclusively. He attacked one of them in the cloakroom with a screwdriver. He was hypnotised.

'He began to offer himself to the older boys. In London he went with random older men who approached him at tube and railway stations. He had learned to see

the need in a stranger's eye. They gave him money, alcohol, drugs. He attended orgies in his school uniform
with important people—'

'Why?'

'His nightmare was not to be recognised. Didn't you
say people go their whole lives wanting to be admired
for their hidden qualities? So look and listen, Waldo,
and learn a lesson. There are many things you don't
know about Eddie.'

We look at one another. I say, 'How long did it go on
for?'

'Four years with Bow.'

'Why did he tell you?'

'In Cannes we had the beach, the moon, the attention.
With us he was top of the world. "This is where I've
always wanted to be – with Waldo, and you, the people
I love most," he said. He sent photos to his kids. "It's
the greatest privilege of my life." But he couldn't enjoy
it – or anything – because he had had something on his
mind for years. He broke down. I had already told him
what had happened to me. So at last he said it.'

'Do any of the women know?'

'He could never mention it. He thought it would
make him hateful. The one person he told was his best
pal, who owns clubs in London. Then me.'

'You're special for him, Zee. Do you know why?'

'Please, Waldo, I can only beg you to zip it right up. Anita must not know this. Or else—'

'Or else?'

'You know.'

I say, 'No need to threaten, Zee. Just tell me, did he see the man after this?'

'Eddie met with Bow in London when he first became a journalist. Bow continued to tell him that he, Eddie, was his greatest creation, that Eddie was smart and charming, he'd never met anyone with more potential. But now he was entirely Bow's invention and project . . .

'Two years later Eddie wrote to Bow, who was living in Bristol. They met several times.

'The past looks worse the closer you look at it. Eddie had started on a round of therapy. Bow insisted to Eddie that he had loved and believed in him. As for the sex, it had been "fun" or "messing around". Not rape.

'Eddie accused the teacher of dirtying every single thing he had, of humiliating him where there should have been care. Hurting him when he was vulnerable, away from his parents. Eddie said he'd been "nothing" to Bow. When he gave himself to other men, he felt like nothing. Even now, a lot of the time, he feels like nothing.

'Eddie returned to Bristol with his friend. Gibbo, I think he's called. They had talked a lot. Gibbo believed that vengeance is the best therapy. He encouraged the man.'

'To what?'

'Recompense Eddie.'

'To give him money, you mean?'

'Otherwise Eddie would make a fuss. The press, the police, utter disgrace and prison even—'

'And the man did?'

'Eddie and Gibbo went to his flat. Eddie demanding, Gibbo threatening. The man's a semi-gangster with a thuggish side. And a cosh. Gibbo poked and tormented him—'

'You can do anything to a guilty man.'

'They carried off cash, a painting and Bow's mother's necklace. All valuable. But Gibbo said it was not enough. They went back.'

'What happened?'

She hesitates. 'Bow was having a breakdown. He babbled on about his charity work. It wasn't pretty. He used the wall. He was bleeding. He wanted to smash his brain in. Gibbo thought it would be a mercy and helped.

'Bow fled the room. They watched him running away. And followed him to the Clifton Suspension Bridge.'

'Did he jump?'

'They saw the body. They returned, took some other things, covered their tracks and sold the stuff. Eddie went to the funeral and then to a railway station, where he was found crouched in a corner, howling and filthy.'

'Eddie killed Bow.'

'The man killed Eddie first. After school, Eddie was mad, unable to get that devil's voice out of his head. He still hears Bow's screams as he fell to his death. But Eddie needed justice.'

'He needed money.'

'They became the same thing.'

'They are not.'

'I hate you trying to be clever, Waldo.'

She has been playing with her jade beads, twisting her hands.

'Do you believe it?'

'I wish I hadn't said anything. I take it back, Waldo. Please—'

'A monster is someone who's been monstered.'

'Oh, shut your silly mouth. You enjoy these things too much. Stop talking or I'll stop you.'

'Aren't you thinking of your reputation? You used to, Zee. What will people say about you – with this man?'

'People? What people?'

Her breathing is shallow and fast. The jade beads break and scatter across the floor like a hailstorm. Rather than reaching down to collect them for fear they will be touched by dirty feet, she snatches up a cushion.

She comes at me. She holds it over my face. She presses it down with her swimmer's arms.

My chest heaves, my legs thrash and twitch. I attempt to strike at her with my fists.

It is like running backwards up stairs. Then there's a break. For a long time I feel as if I'm underwater, drowning.

When I come to, she is crouching on the floor, breathing hard, staring at me.

I wonder who she has turned into and what sort of madness this is.

'Why did you make me, Waldo? You – you with your unreasonableness. You asked for it. You even paid Eddie to disappear—'

'I did?'

'That was a filthy thing to do behind my back. You made me hand him money.'

'He begged me to pay his rent.'

'He's gone because of you.'

'He'll be back when he's horny and hungry.'

'God, you could make a woman extreme . . .'

She reaches for my arm. I offer my hand. She will comfort me. But she is pulling me. She is dragging me out of my chair. I will end up on the floor.

'Come on, old man – come and get me, if you want me!'

It all stops. She has put her finger to her lips.

'No – pipe down. Stop panting in that doglike way.' We are quiet. 'There's someone at the door.'

'Yes, I'm afraid I think I can hear the buzzer.'

'Waldo, silence!' We wait. 'Yes, it's true. There's someone there. Someone wants us.'

SEVEN

Eddie has returned after four days. With a slight tan, I notice. The weather can be wild in Brighton. He grins uncomfortably and hops from foot to foot.

He sighs. 'Sorry, busy with the kids.'

'Why didn't you call?'

I say, 'We were about to call the police.'

'Why? Never do that. I lost my phone. Then I found it again. And you missed me! I'm glad to be home.'

They need to talk, and swipe me into in a corner of the room, where I draw, play with images on my iPad, and listen to the music I'm using through my headphones. I am like an aged ape in a suspended cage in the corner, unable to even spit at the guests.

They hurry me to bed. He is staying the night. I can hear her feet rushing across the floor.

I address the camera I have had rigged up in the corner of my room, the one which will watch me die. I turn off my hearing aid and take two pills. Still I can hear her distressed voice in the night, calling out in Punjabi. He comforts her; she is soon quiet.

*

In the morning she feeds Eddie before he leaves for a meeting in his new clothes and my shoes.

While she waits, Zee arranges fresh flowers. You see people truly when they enjoy the most. Today the world is an apple Zee wants to bite into. There is music, a little dancing and much clattering in cupboards. She puts away her clothes, rearranges her dresses, folds her sweaters, discards lingerie. She sorts out her 'important' shoes and takes some to the charity shop. Photographs are moved.

When Eddie returns she goes to greet him. They sit close together. I listen. I learn they have a plan. It stimulates them like an amphetamine.

She starts to pack. Rapture tears down the walls of habit. This is how they will live when I'm dead.

My highly honed skills – the look, the sulk, the sigh, the silence – aren't working. I have been disappeared. I cannot stay in my hole like an animal, fearing myself.

I wheel into her room and catch her, reminding her that I am still here.

'You're going to Paris? Zee. Please answer me.'

'On the next train.'

'Without me?'

'There's no time to organise.'

'Where are you staying?'

'The Ritz.'

'That's where we had our anniversary.'

'It's convenient.'

'How will you afford it?'

'Shut up.'

'And even after what we said about his character?'

'Jealousy is a despicable thing. Didn't you always tell me so? We're developing a business idea. Don't you like me as an independent woman? Eddie has some contacts who will invest in us. His French is perfect; he never yells. People believe in him. You will hear about the project.'

'When?'

She says, 'When you stop watching me like that. I shiver when I feel your eyes on me.'

'I'll look the other way.'

'We're in a rush. Please remove yourself before I trip over you.' I sit there with a head like a glowing cigarette. 'You'll burst, Waldo. This is self-inflicted.'

She puts on her large Greta Garbo sunglasses before slipping into her heels.

'What would your mother say, Zee?'

'Don't you dare, Waldo.'

'We should talk about it.'

'Not now. You're holding me back.'

She walks out with Eddie.

'What a happy couple they are,' says the nurse who comes in as they leave. 'Is he your son?'

I don't even laugh. I look away and I ask the nurse to remain silent and still my bleating heart with a pot of lapsang and a jug of boiling water on the side.

I don't like being left for long struggling with my dangerous self. I am more compassionate when Zee – my friend, ally, pal – can hear me. Thoughts, unconverted into words, can become monstrous, like heavy metal in your head. The world can seem very strange when there are no words for experience. But there is music. There is Muddy Waters. Nothing consoles like the blues. Muddy knows what I'm going through. He's seen it all.

I discover that Zee has taken a chunk of money from our joint account. It was only I who put anything in it: earnings from royalties and sometimes from talks, appearances or teaching work at the film school. I've not only been abandoned: I'm paying for these moon-eyed sweethearts to stay at the Ritz, and all I can hope for is that she brings me an ashtray.

I was a serene old man treading the nirvanic plateau to oblivion. Now I wake up, wanting love, seething, seeing her mouth drawing in his cock, over and over. I've become a disgruntled father rather than a lover or friend. I can't bear not to be on her mind.

I need talk. I need advice. I need the cavalry.

I call Anita. Anita is my other girl.

Anita loves secrets and gossip. She will know what to do. She will have good ideas. When she hears this, she will be on fire.

EIGHT

Anita is not a woman a man can look at for long without wanting to put his penis in her mouth. My eyes take in her hair, cheekbones, fine hands. I close my eyes and bask in her voice as she reads to me.

For months Anita Bassett has been visiting at least once a fortnight. She began reading me classical texts. Being a movie and theatre star, her voice is a caress from God.

Anita was in three of my films. I worked out how to photograph her, letting her be witty, wicked, amusing. With Anita it's a one-woman show: she communicates directly with an audience. As a director, all you could do was set it up and sit back. These were her best performances, some say.

She does charity work with children; she reads, lunches and appears on chat shows; she rests in her small house on a cliff near Amalfi, learning Italian. In London she comes to me with a large bunch of my favourite flowers: thistles.

Some people pay to hear her speak. Nothing made me

fall asleep faster, so we made a new arrangement. She brings me ganja. And when she sits on my couch, her hair in a ponytail, with her lovely knees drawn up, she reads to me from my favourite detective stories, ones I loved as a kid. As a reader, I'm done with literature. I only want fun.

Her kindness temporarily releases me from my fury. I am in a good place until my eyes fall on Eddie's stuff tucked behind the end of the other sofa, across the room.

Anita's voice has stopped. She has been watching me.

'Is all well, Waldo? Am I too dull for you today? You want a little song? How about a twerk?'

'You're the only person left. I trust you completely.'

She puts the book down. 'What about Zee?'

'This concerns her. Will you tell me the truth without restraint? What sort of man is Eddie, that pal of mine who visits all the time? My estimation of things might be off. Reality can be precarious. Now it has begun to curve and bend—'

'It has?'

'Eddie Warburten, he's a public-school flâneur, a sort of gigolo. Recently he has moved right in on us. He makes love to Zee—'

'Here?'

'In this apartment. In her bedroom. If they are rushed, even in the living room.'

'You allow it? Waldo – really? But you are – you can be – a brute.'

'Thanks.'

'What's going on?'

'Zee has fallen for him. She was always something of a fantasist. She is relatively young. He gives her hope and cock. She will go crazy if I break them apart. She insists he travel with us. They leave me to stew while they see the sights with their arms around one another. It is as if she has released an enormous rat into my apartment.'

Far from the sympathy and fury I expected, Anita regards me with bizarre scepticism.

'You're being silly, Waldo. Zee adored you from the moment you met. You're not an easy person, believe me. Think carefully, dear friend, before you accuse her.'

'I'm a deluded mad old man?'

'Your mind resembles a roaring wind tunnel. You told me yourself, darling. Let's have a drink and forget all this. Red or white?'

I say, 'Eddie and I were once sitting with an elderly woman. Perhaps in her eighties. He took her hand and caressed it with both his hands while looking into her eyes. She was his forever. It was so moving and effective. Then he tells the women he was sexually abused. It's an aphrodisiac, baby. Makes them so crazy to help they give him all their money. He has done this to Zee.'

'Do you have any evidence, Waldo?' I look at her again. 'Think of the numerous drugs you have to take and what they can do.'

I tell her the story. She does me the credit of listening well.

'But there's no actual evidence, Waldo.'

I'm getting mad. 'I've explained everything. You're saying I'm ridiculous and he's a saint?'

'We need more than this to go on.'

'You don't believe the barefaced truth?'

'Don't torment yourself, Waldo. It would be a terrible thing to accuse Zee. On the other hand – doesn't a woman need a little pleasure?' She kisses me and prepares to leave. 'Don't be glum.' At the door, she stops and turns. 'I can do something. I could have him checked out. It won't take any time at all.'

'How?'

'I'll get my assistant onto it. He'll make a report. Then we can decide whether to fatwa the dog – if he is a dog. After all, a saint is only someone who has been under-researched.'

'There's one more thing. Would you do something?'

'Ask.'

'Please pull out that stuff. Over there.' I indicate Eddie's things.

'Are you sure?'

'You said "anything".'

'I'm too kind.'

'Bring it to me, then.'

'I'll do it for you, Waldo.'

She goes over, pulls his bags out and tips the stuff onto the floor. I nod. She picks through it, showing me everything.

There are dirty clothes, shoes and toiletries. Computer drives and wires. Condoms and a cock ring. A small capsule filled with blue Viagra pills. A tube of lubricant. A vibrator. Two mobile phones, a camera, two expensive watches. Expensive cufflinks. The manuscript of a novel. Panties, a book of matches from a smart restaurant and three 'Dear Dad' letters from 'F' – his daughter Francesca, I guess – which I cannot bear to read.

'Look more. Poke about.'

'Yuck.'

'Go in there, please. I'll buy you a manicure.'

In the inside pocket of a bag she finds a frayed, shambolic diary held together by a rubber band.

'Open it, please.'

Business cards, newspaper cuttings and photographs of children fall out. A wad of twenties: about £300. And something I read: two local newspaper articles about Bow's suicide.

She is looking at a photograph. She shields her eyes. She says, 'I wonder, Waldo, if this is – er – anyone you know.'

I reach for it. She holds onto it. Then hands it to me: a printed selfie. An older woman on her knees in stockings and heels, with dildos in her arse and cunt.

'I'm sorry, Waldo. Those shoes—'

'She was in her room a lot, with the door closed.'

'This is harsh.' She says, 'There are more. Can you bear to see them?'

I make copies with my phone. There's no justice when it comes to sex. We're all pornographers now.

'She's become crazed,' I say. 'Could you please read the diary to me.'

'I feel odd. This is becoming repulsive.'

She reads from Eddie's diary. He's no Pepys – meetings, walks, character sketches, ideas for articles and documentaries, notes on my obituary where he is complimentary but dismisses two of the better films. I soon get it. Nothing incriminating about Zee.

She lets me be silent for a while. A good friend can do this. Anita could be right: folly can flatten everything good in a moment.

I have an idea.

'Can you do something else? Photograph the pages so I can read and reread at my leisure.'

She makes a face. But she extracts her phone and does it. She emails me the material so I can read it on my iPad later while pretending to be dead.

I hear the front door downstairs slam. The lift clanks. 'It's them, Anita.'

The diary is in my lap. In a panic I drop it. Eddie's stuff slides over the floor. Anita moves quickly, picking up everything and replacing it as best she can. She hurries into the bathroom to wash her hands.

One of the photographs has fallen face down on the floor. I wheel over but however I strain I cannot pick it up. I try to kick it under the sofa and almost fall out of my chariot. I think of throwing a cushion over it, but there isn't time now.

Eddie and Zee come in.

'Hey, you two,' I say. 'How was Paris? Look – I have a friend visiting. See who it is. Come and say hi. Let's have tea. Let's open champagne. Bring cake.'

NINE

I say, 'See what I do for you, Eddie?'

Suddenly Eddie opens his arms, he is so excited to see Anita walking towards him. His eyes vibrate with excitement.

'You are my Marilyn.'

'Boo-boo be-doo.'

Anita kisses Eddie, kisses Zee. She begins to work Eddie, her words all over him. I photograph them together.

'I have to hear it all,' Anita tells him. 'Tell me everything about yourself.' This is a subject he is mad for. She says, 'I must go and rehearse soon – but come on.'

She offers her hand, inviting him to join her in the kitchen for a brandy.

He hurries, almost tripping over. 'Won't be long.' He stops, picks up the photograph and looks at it. 'This is a picture of my daughter Francesca.' He examines us. 'Why is it here?'

'You must have dropped it.'

'I'm certain I didn't.'

He looks at us again, puts it back among his things, and Anita shuts the door.

It is quiet. Zee and I are excluded. But we are together. She squats down beside me for the first time in weeks. I watch her make a cigarette, insert the filter, lick it, light it and smoke it.

'What are they chatting about, do you think? Why is she talking to him like this?'

'He must be telling her the names of everyone famous he's met. He's watched her in the theatre for more than twenty-five years. Her leather-and-fur *Duchess of Malfi* helped make him the man he is.'

'For Christ's sake, Waldo, she won't want to hear that. These filmi girls are praised everywhere.'

'Maybe she sees in him what you do.'

'Like what?'

I say, 'Boring people are always popular. They never do anything unexpected. But he has a keenness. Some enthusiasm. Ardour. What else? Let me ponder. It's a big subject.'

She pours herself a large glass of wine.

'Don't be ridiculous. How is it that she comes round every time I go out?'

'You know I don't like to be left alone. Her beauty cheers me up.'

She says, 'But what are the two of them doing in there?'

'We can ask Eddie later. If he's around. Can we be together tonight, baby, or will he be joining us this evening?'

'He will be.'

'How was Paris? Did you go to the Avenue Montaigne, and were the young people lovely? Was it productive?'

'I'll tell you in good time.'

'Would you get me a drink?'

'Sure.'

'Are there any olives?'

'I bought some the other day.'

'My favourites?'

'Your favourites.'

'You haven't forgotten me.'

'You're unforgettable, Waldo.'

'Kiss me.'

She slaps my face with her open hand.

'Ouch. Why? You've bruised my lip. Kiss it better, baby.'

'You know what you've been doing. I'll get you some wine. Soon you won't feel a thing.'

Being beaten, being loved, what's the difference? I smile and watch her. I love to look at her, the way she moves and does things.

'Anita won't seduce him, Zee. She has class.'

'She's been through a lot of men but none of them seemed to stick. Why is that?'

I shrug. 'She has high standards.'

'She still has "that thing".'

'What, Zee? Charm?'

'Seductiveness and a touch of masochism.'

'So do you still have it, Zee. But you're losing it.'

'How?'

'You're in a hurry now. Charm is slow. It makes time. It's languid and confident. Artists, sportsmen – Zidane, Miles Davis, Garbo – and the people I like best. They have it. Slowness. Infinitude.'

She puts the drink beside me and rolls another cigarette. She watches herself in the mirror, turning her head from side to side.

'Look – this horrible mirror hates me. Why do you have to have them everywhere?

'You bring her here and didn't even warn me that she was coming. One of the most beautiful women in the world. You can tell a healthy woman by her skin.

'Have you noticed she never wears cheap shoes, even with jeans? She's never without that Prada bag. The other day at the exhibition she didn't wear a bra. Who would dare at her age? Faultless all the time. It kills me. You were right—'

'About what?'

Zee pulls at her face. 'You know only the myth matters. How things seem to others. Look at me. I'm tiny. I'm even Indian. My nose shines. How could you treat me like this today?'

'Anita is my talking book. That's all. You know you excite me . . .'

'Touch my dry hair.'

'Let me put coconut in it for you.'

'Look at my withered hands. These varicose veins here in my legs have to be removed. My knees are arthritic. When we went to that dinner the other day at Bafta, I felt like the oldest woman there. Not one person looked at me. Didn't I mesmerise men, once?'

'Particularly me.'

'They chased me but I ignored them. I was a prude and called it feminism.'

I say, 'It's only in the movies that people are beautiful all the time.'

She says, 'Does every woman have my fear? That I'll turn into my mother?'

'Don't traduce her, Zee. Your Bibi was a fascinating woman who could look at herself without fear. I remember her praying. It moved me so to see it, Zee. One time she let me join her. She urged me to convert. She said we had got it all wrong in the West. And you should have gone to Pakistan.'

'She wanted that? Absurd.'

'We've lost our relationship to truth and value. We've become slaves—'

'To what?'

'Brief passions. Sex fantasies. Money. Time in London passed too quickly for her. She said one could become old in a day.'

Zee is silent. She walks about.

'How could you listen to that? I admit you were patient. You were kind with the children and you were kind with her. Mum was old at forty, and too devout,' she says. 'You helped me break away. Suppose tomorrow I discover I have cancer? Everything could change in a moment. I want a new nose. Will you get me one?'

'If you ask me right.' I sip my whisky. 'I was thinking of getting a new penis at the same time.'

She sits with her head in her hands.

'Anita doesn't have a boyfriend, does she? Didn't you say she'd never found the love of her life?'

'She broke up with one of my scribblers. A bastard I thrashed into talent. She claims that no one dares ask her on dates, except younger men.'

'I know what you say to women, Waldo. You say she is too intelligent for most men.'

'She is sharp, she's mischievous. She's sexual. She regrets many things – not having a family. With men she sought punishment.'

Zee paces. 'She is a danger. You're crafty: you brought her here on purpose. Don't you talk to her about me? What do you say?'

'I say you make me unhappy.'

'You said that? Does she have any idea what it's like to look after someone day and night for years? Let her try. Does she have a husband who messes the bed? I know how your mind works and so I have to slap you. Why are they taking so long?'

'Only because he's telling her about himself. What a famous producer he was. How he lost it because of someone else. How he'll be getting it back. How he'll be investing in her new movie. How he'll be—'

She covers her ears. 'Shut up!'

When Anita leaves, Zee takes Eddie into her bedroom. I can't hear the details; they are arguing. Their voices low. She goes down on him. He's not a man to waste an erection. At his age you can't, I'm telling you. His semen is better than bubbly.

They emerge to clean their palates with a nice Chablis. I try to catch Eddie's eye, but he keeps his distance.

That evening Zee is excited. She wants to talk to me. The business idea isn't bad. They will do it together. She calls it her 'baby'. Eddie inspires her. She wants more.

It is our destiny to feel forever deprived of something. The world I offer her is too small, and she is keen to start something new. Don't I know that feeling? What do I, an old man, have to offer any woman now?

I notice she has returned with her hair loose, her skirts tight and new perfumes. She has an ankle brace-let and a leather jacket. I'd like to see her naked, except for the black jacket, perhaps with spike heels. Definitely with rouged lips. Right now wouldn't be a good time to propose such a pose.

I lie in bed looking at the selfies my wife sent to her lover. Then I text Anita. 'Any news?' And again, 'Am black as hell here. What's going on?'

Nothing.

TEN

Anita doesn't reply the next day. Or the next. Four days pass. I'm worried. I text her. She doesn't get back to me. Has she gone away? Is she wildly busy?

My confidence is dented but it hasn't disappeared. With my iPad on my lap, I study the photographs of Eddie's diary. I am shocked by how little he earns and how often he goes to the doctor. When he makes love he puts a tick. I like an organised man. If I had a future, I'd do that myself.

I watch. I haven't seen my own feet for years. I can see my reflection in the mirror. I asked the maid to move it. If she turns it a little so that the mirrors can exchange glances, I can lie down and see into my theatre – the living room – even as I record. Many movies feature voyeurs, and I am perfect for the part, with James Stewart's patience. Many other movies, I recall, feature our other neighbour, the serial killer.

The next morning, while Zee is on the running machine, I notice, as I wheel myself about the place, other alterations. Eddie is moving into my office. He places

my files and Sundance award on a shelf in the hall behind the coats. He puts my notebooks and storyboards
into a box. He moves my sketchbooks and my Peter
Blake print.

When he is done with the removals, he sits down and
works at his phone and computer, his DVDs and books
next to him, his rat-tail throbbing with excitement.

They are becoming more careless. For the last few
days I've left my iPad on the sideboard, with the video
camera running. They forget it's there, and walk in and
out of the frame, talking as I snooze.

Later, I lie in bed watching it.

I hear her voice. 'Waldo never comes in here . . . He
never uses these things . . . He never will again . . . He's
holding everything up . . . It's like living in a museum . . .
He's too drunk to notice . . . Do you notice how he hogs
the vodka? We've got to get on – what does he want
space for? He hardly remembers the films he's made.
I'm not sure how strong he is now—'

'It's true the poor man's in a bad way. If he was a dog
he'd be put down. He said the other day, "I may be due
a one-way ticket to Switzerland"—'

'Buy it, please, Eddie, dear. He can barely breathe as
it is.'

Their yoga teacher arrives. Zee and Eddie meditate
together, practising 'belly breathing'. Emptiness doesn't

come cheap. While seeing Eddie do the 'downward dog' is its own reward, there is the bonus of hearing them discuss the nature of cosmic happiness. This resides in the moment rather than materialism. Zee informs Eddie that he is too left-brained. Something in him has been frozen by trauma. Zee wants the teacher to help him. Together they can bring that part of him back to life. It will benefit everyone, accelerate fat loss, boost brain-power and increase mental clarity.

When Zee is not in search of vacuity, she sits next to Eddie on the sofa with her new computer. She also bought Eddie a new MacBook Pro. Salmon, vodka, cakes, steaks, wine, champagne arrive from Harrods. We have picnics in the front room on damask throws. We are living the high life. In the afternoon they have massages. He has never been more relaxed, he tells her. No woman has done so much for him.

My nights are empty. I cannot even masturbate.

He takes her to the theatre and to the opera. They go backstage, where he introduces her to the actors in their dressing rooms. There's dinner after and good wine. He knows the best places and makes the bookings with her credit card.

Spending my money isn't an effort for him. They go to the V&A for lunch. A bit of shopping in South Kensington after. The flat fills up with curtains, carpets, cushions, bed linen. She's started buying prints. They're expensive: thousands of pounds each. She can't believe we've been so deprived while others have so much. And Eddie: he is one of the finest men that money can buy.

She's getting changed and talks to him in the living room. Hidden by the crimson drapes, I am not here but motionless on the terrace watching the neighbours.

When Zee gets agitated, her voice is loud. If I switch on my hearing aid and lean back, I get the idea.

'It's been rough, Eddie, you sweetheart. Pour me a white wine, will you? Until recently I'd hardly been out because of you-know-who, and you know what a damn chatterbox I am.'

'You have friends. You're always at lunch gossiping with nice people.'

'Dull old women with their cancers, talking about illnesses, funerals and wills, and none of them with all their original organs. Someone is always dying, and no one charms me. Until you, Eddie, there was nothing.'

'I thought you'd be too snobbish to be interested in me.'

'Why? Waldo's been ill for ten years. At one point, when he broke his arm falling over, I was doing all the cooking; cutting up his food and feeding him before putting him to bed.

'He never liked to be left alone. He got depressed, sad and cruel. He's was a pervert – anything normal bored him. I refused to urinate on him but he made me spit on him. I liked that.'

'I can see why. I do it to people whenever I can.'

'He taught me gaiety. He said, "Be sure to do something new in sex every time." I can't satisfy his lusts. You can't love someone your whole life, can you? Have you done that?'

'No.'

'Before you, I had a dream over and over,' she continues, 'that someone was holding my hand. One evening I saw you looking at my hands. You reached over and stroked me. It was lovely, but I wondered if you thought they were veined and withered. I was too old for love. It's gone.'

'But you texted me.'

'I did! It took the courage of Boadicea. I was so ashamed and nervous. I wanted to throw my phone away.'

'I apologise, but I didn't see you like that, Zee. Forward with men. What was it you said? That if I wanted you I could have you.'

'I'd never kissed a man before he kissed me. I dithered for days. I changed my mind over and over. I thought you'd reject me. I was in a state. I was so relieved when you sent me that picture of your mouth making a kiss that I cried.

'Now be truthful with me, Eddie. Have you ever been faithful to any woman?'

There is a pause. 'Not yet.'

'Why not? Is infidelity a belief or an instinct?'

'Sex is the only time I don't have anxiety, and can forget myself. I am at peace briefly, and my mind is not full of hate and noise. Everything falls into place.' Then he says, 'Sweetheart, what do you want?'

'I wanted to live in America. I begged Waldo, to be near the girls and the grandchild. He said they didn't want us around all the time. Their husbands would rebel. It became all the same here – dullsville. Dying is hard work and takes so long.'

'You told me he's fascinating.'

'Once it was a whirl. But I became a carer in my fifties. It was my duty and my love. I wanted him to have a wonderful last decade. But I was trapped. I would sit with him, that penis in a wheelchair—'

'Please—'

'—looking out of the window. And I'd start to shake. Like a palsy. My therapist said it was claustrophobia. I was getting fat too . . .

'My friends said I was lucky to get out of India. Pakistan – where my husband was headed – would have been worse. Waldo took me away. That was kind. He saved me. I have to love him for that.'

'Do you?'

'I'm grateful. I have everything here. How can I complain . . . ? Oh, Eddie, do you see what I mean?'

'I do, I do.'

'Waldo didn't want me to work. He liked me with him. Together we went through his scripts, the costumes, editing, music. He asked me about everything and even nodded his head and looked thoughtful, and changed things if I suggested it. Now he never even shows me his photographs or little films.'

'You want to see them?'

'Of course. And he prefers to have Anita read to him. Do you find me boring, Eddie?'

'Not at all.'

She kisses him. 'I hope you're less afraid and more relaxed since we had the massages and paid off that last bastard, the landlord. I can't believe he shoved a sweetie like you against a wall and threatened you in that squalid corridor. Let me kiss you again.'

I endure this pause.

He says, 'I was desperate, but I came clean. I admitted what I did. I forged something and it annoyed him.'

'That's all in the past. You'll never have to do that with me by your side. How long did you have to live there?'

'Three, no, four years.'

'He wouldn't dare touch me. I'd have kicked him in the balls. And all that for just a few thousand pounds.'

'You know I have other debts?'

'Didn't I promise all will be taken care of, in time?' She laughs. 'Are you going to give up your other women for me? Your "ladies-in-waiting"?'

'There are none now, darling.'

'You'll be surprised, Eddie, but I can be very fierce. One day I'll tell you my family history. Come and hold me in your strong arms, baby.'

I sit there, frozen, struggling to remember where I am until they're done with their hugging and fondling and come fetch me.

Then I see a text from Anita.

ELEVEN

I have a cold and am draped in several blankets like a broken sofa. But at least Anita has got back to me.

She brings news of the fabulous fabulist. We must talk. She is coming straight over. She has organised a picnic. A driver will take us to the Serpentine, which was one of my favourite places to loaf and goof as a young man.

It is a lovely day, and the park is crowded. The lake shimmers. I like to see people cycling, roller-skating, lying in the sun. This is London: peaceful, pleasure-loving. I enjoy her pushing me. The water calms me. Anita wears cropped jeans with gold sandals, a white T-shirt, big sunglasses and a hat. Still she is recognised and never fails to smile gratefully and keep her head down.

I'm hoping for a last outing in a pedalo.

She finds us a pool of shadow and we sit together eating smoked salmon sandwiches and drinking champagne.

'Sorry it took so long.' She's serious and concentrating. 'There was a lot. I was surprised.'

'You believe me now?'

'My boys and their slaves were busy. You've got it going on, Waldo. I was waiting to see what we had. If it was real.'

I turn to her as much as I can. I catch a glimpse of her face. The truth is not deep. It is not even hidden. It is just unbearable. 'One must dare all things with women,' Stendhal advises. I've long known Eddie was capable of taking liberties. It is in his nature, as a dog must piss against trees.

'Anita, push me into the water. Watch me go down and hold my head under if I kick. I don't want to hear more. I love Zee. I can't help it. She's a little naive and I'm not sure I can protect her from this man. Or if she wants me to.'

I explain that there are, as I've gathered from the diary, at least two other women at the moment, along with several from the past who still take an interest in him. I find ten women's names under his 'keep in touch' list. Love is consuming work. Eddie is generous with his time. He gives the women a lot of himself. No wonder he never finished or indeed started his 'definitive' history of British post-war cinema, not something which would take anyone more than a weekend to knock out.

I inform Anita of this. She nods, impressed. Now it is her turn. On her side, as she says, her people have been busy and thorough, and she has a clipboard. There are several pages. With photographs.

She begins. 'You confirm our work. The most significant is a widow called Patricia Howard. She has had a mastectomy and been alone for five years. She's keen to be loved. She is hot and wealthy, but has three grown-up children who are suspicious of Eddie and protective of their mother.

'He's persistent, as you know. He keeps it going, talks to her every day and sits through Wagner for her. He even reads her novels and gives her advice.'

'That is commitment.'

'Indeed. He is hoping she will forward him some money to make one into a film – directed by him. He has slept with her but can't make a move to a more permanent arrangement. I'm not sure he will – he's afraid of her children.'

'Go on.'

'There's another one, Sarah Adler, twenty-eight. An artist, mad as a cut snake, his favourite fuck.'

I take the clipboard and look at some Facebook photographs of her.

'There they are together at the opening of her art show.'

I say, 'When he claimed to be in Brighton.'

'She has a beautiful body with delicious breasts that

she likes to have pegged. She wears a pretty chain be-tween her tits. She talks and he listens, which is unusual with men. She is dependent, and threatens suicide once a month. She sucks him off better than anyone ever has.'

'I hope my wife doesn't get to hear about this.'

'Sarah was the woman he disappeared with. He promised to help her with her show and she held him to it. But apparently he was anxious that day. He was shuffling and making guttural noises, which alarmed the gallery owners . . .

'We tracked down another woman who had a scene with him. She had made him a considerable loan so he could research a documentary on you.'

'I think a documentary on Eddie would be more inter-esting.'

'She'd have come to your place. She wants her money back. Failing that, she couldn't wait to give us the dope. Wait for this. If you want to hear about his virtues—'

'I've never been keener.'

'Eddie is known as a prodigious cunnilinguist. He is the Jacques Cousteau of pussy work. He can stay down there for hours without breathing. He gave her crabs.'

'What's his technique with the women?'

'He deals in futures. And hope. He tells them how beautiful and intelligent they are. They'll live together in New York or Rio. They will start a business. They will eat lovely food, talk lovely words, and make lovely love for the rest of their lives.'

'Are people so easily fooled?'

'They flee the truth like Ebola. I don't need to tell you.'

'Yes, and as with all movies which feature detectives or investigative journalists, we only learn the truth when it is too late.' I say to her, 'I know women like to be talked into love. Doesn't Othello do that to Desdemona? I envy Eddie's agile tongue, Anita. I hate the fact I've grown impotent – even in my hate.'

'Waldo, you had better locate your mojo.'

'Is there a rush?'

'At the suggestion of his close pal Gibbo, Eddie is hiding out at your place. I think he will squeeze you. Eddie needs a big steal, Waldo. He's been bankrupt twice. He doesn't have a credit card or chequebook. We discovered he owes money everywhere. To the government in taxes, to his wives, one of whom has cancer and can't work. The children are difficult.'

'What's the situation there?'

'One girl disabled. The older boy is psychotic – anyhow, off the planet. He's on a locked ward.

'Another boy lives in Italy. The one Eddie loves most is his daughter in her mid-teens. But she is difficult, to say the least. Demanding, when it comes to money. More?'

'Please.'

'Years of this sadness made Eddie more off-beam. Even shits want to be good fathers. He spent thousands on doctors, psychiatrists, therapists of all kinds for his kids and for himself. There isn't a quack in the land who could turn off the noise in his head. Or resist his money. Even he has had more hands on him than Linda Lovelace.

'Eddie has borrowed widely for years. He owes money to his friends, to the banks, to landlords and film producers. He's being pursued by bailiffs. He has nothing to his name and wants something. If a person wants to take you, if they are determined, they can strip someone of their soul, even.'

As far as I'm concerned, we need less action and more whining. I say, 'Doesn't a man deserve peace at this time of his life? Surely, if she wants a broken man, what's wrong with me?'

'Don't weep.' She takes my hand. 'She wants to see how you will deal with it. She wants you to pull her back from him. Perhaps your demands have become weak. What is a husband for?'

'Sorry?'

She almost yells at me. 'To protect a woman from herself. Now, let jealousy be your spur.'

'It will be, Anita.'

She pushes me around the pond. We stop to pick up coffee. We are quiet except for the ticking of my wheels. I talk to myself, as usual.

But she leans towards me. 'What did you say, Waldo? Are you mumbling?'

'I said at least she has someone.'

'Zee? What do you mean?'

'She hasn't remained passive. She took something she wanted.'

'You admire that?'

At the end of his essay 'The Theme of the Three Caskets', Freud says of us, 'It is in vain that an old man yearns for the love of a woman as he had it first from his mother.' Yet I know of several old men in various states of decay or dissolution – inevitably the worst men, who behaved most badly towards women – who have found youngish, angelic women to walk them to the gate of darkness. Saintly, useful, kind: these keepers of the phallus don't mind at all. They like it. There's no accounting for taste.

'Are you dating?'

'I wish,' she sighs. 'It's been too long. Men come on to me, but they're all twenty-five. I went with one or other of them a few times. None of them have got "that thing". I'm ready to give up on it all, Waldo. Who would tolerate me?'

'I can't hear you say that, baby. Are you working on it?'

'I'm helping you right now, Waldo. I'm concerned about what you'll do with this information about Eddie. Swear to me you'll be careful. Use it sparingly. You don't want to blow her up. Or yourself.'

'I know this, Anita. Zee is lost in a fantasy. Sexual ecstasy only lasts a few weeks. Soon she will know what he is really like. She won't be able to disregard it. I'm counting the minutes – and you and I will hurry the process along. You've given me the opening I was looking for.'

Who'd have thought retirement would be so apocalyptic?

I am weak and unhappy but I haven't given up. I plan my next move.

Dynamite or not, it will be direct and radical, I'm telling you. If she is not ready to give up on love, she must be made ready.

I don't want her to be happy. I just want her to be with me. Is that too much to ask?

TWELVE

'Do you think he doesn't have other women? That he is not with Patricia Howard?'

'Who?'

'Her. Don't look away.'

'This is like an assault. It's cruel. Do I need to see this?'

'It would be a good idea.'

'Why?'

'It'll help you.'

'Now you are shoving it in my face. Get away.'

'Please.'

We are alone. I have prepared. There is a picture of Patricia on my iPad, which I offer to her. Pat was married to a well-known actor I once employed.

Zee takes the iPad. I study her face as she looks. Despite the dangers involved, I am keen, as the truth-doctor, to relieve my wife of her ignorance. A strong dose of reality will lead to a renewal of our love. She will return to me. All will be well once more.

I say, 'She is nice-looking. Don't you think? Usually Eddie goes for less attractive women. They are more grateful, as he once explained.

'Patricia has "helped him out" – cufflinks, watches, a computer, phones, tickets to Wimbledon, and so on. Her husband was a well-known theatre actor.'

'So?'

'Patricia was in a position to introduce Eddie to useful people. She loaned him money to "tide him over". He didn't return it. She wasn't surprised, and anyhow, he listens to her heroically, and how many women can find such an ear? He makes demands, subtly. He knows how to do this. You have to admire someone who has no integrity. I certainly do. But still . . .'

Zee is pulling her hair out, strand by strand. She picks up a pillow and holds it out. She presses it into her face, to see how long she can last. She is red-faced and breathing hard.

Satisfied by her experiment, she approaches me. 'Of course any intelligent, desirable man would have entanglements. Charm does that. It goes without saying. Didn't you do the same? I've heard about it from all sorts.'

'No.'

'No?'

She regards me with some calculation, as if about to guess my measurements. She bites her lip, concentrating. Then she pushes the cushion over my face and holds it there. This is the longest it has been. I try to kick out at her, but at last I go limp. She doesn't flinch. She looks at me and continues. She's not having any nonsense.

When it stops she says, 'Anything else?'

I am shuddering uncontrollably. I gasp, 'Wait.'

'Carry on, Waldo. Do your worst. Let's see if I can take it.'

I feel as if I have run a long way. I gather my breath. Her eyes are hard. She waits.

'Don't you see, he's not in our reality, Zee. He'll meet a woman, fall in love after five minutes, and drive her to Prague the next day to try to buy a castle – with her money.'

'Who doesn't admire spontaneity?'

'He's a psycho, Zee. Only madmen are free. But listen to me—'

'Who isn't mad? He's made some mistakes, I agree.'

'Mistakes? There's another girl. The sculptress.' Lovers endure a servitude that slaves would baulk at. But this might shift her. 'You want to know about it?'

'Will you never die? How you torment me.'

'With the truth.'

'I doubt it's that.'

I say, 'Look at this one. Sarah and Eddie at her gallery opening.

'And what a voluptuous, long-legged minx she is, Zee.

101

She loves her breasts being slapped, pulled and pegged. She begs him to be vicious. Can you do that for him? I worry you might be too tender for Eddie. The minx makes him go further than he has with any woman before. She was the woman he was with when he disappeared with our money and you went out looking for him.'

She covers her face. 'Christ, Waldo, I thought you'd calmed down with age.'

'Zee, can I have a glass of water?'

'This is not the Ritz and I'm not a servant.'

'You'll be relieved to hear he's on dangerous ground with the minx.'

'How?'

'Her father has found out. He will remove Eddie's nuts unless he makes himself scarce. You are his best hope. That's why he clings so.'

'I see.'

'I hope you haven't touched him. I'm sorry you have to be celibate. But I'm telling you, Eddie's used to making a whore of himself. You told me yourself. He has no standards. He's riddled with sexual disease.'

Her mouth opens wide. 'How do you think you know this?'

'I have contacts.'

'Where?'

'All I can say is we are in danger, baby. We must get him out of here and go back to where we were.' I stop. 'But I don't feel like talking now, Zee. I've said enough. I'm weak and my throat is dry.'

She fetches a glass of water and throws it over me. She holds the pillow over my face. My chest will explode. My bloodless head spins.

Then she is done. She goes to make a cup of tea for us both.

She is weeping. 'Look what you've done to me, Waldo. What a fucking bastard you are with your tales.'

'This is a lovely cup of tea, Zee.'

She is rubbing her forehead.

'Waldo, I don't feel well.'

'What's up? Tell me, baby.'

'Oh, I don't know, Waldo. My head is steaming. Everything is getting too much.'

She rolls and smokes a cigarette and I watch her.

'Oh God, oh God, oh God, Waldo.'

'You need rest, baby,' I say. 'Killing me is wearing you out.'

THIRTEEN

Ill and sulking, she looks like a bomb site. Fatigue, headaches, vomiting, the skin under her eyes is violet. She sleeps in her overcoat when she is like this and won't eat or even drink. She refuses to look at us. She's either taken a Valium or two, or she's had it with us. Both, probably.

Eddie has just come in, and he looks at her and then at me over and over. He can't work out what has changed. He believed they were going to the Wolseley for oysters and a night of love.

He shuffles about, flapping his hands. If he isn't fondling my wife he doesn't know where to put them.

She knows what she wants tonight. She goes into her room and shuts the door, taking a bottle of wine with her. That, from her point of view, is that. I pity her, flung into the threshing machine of desire, unable to escape. After the delivery of my report on Eddie, it will take a few days of mourning and regret for her to feel stronger.

Not only am I succeeding here, but I can now humiliate Eddie. It will help him learn from his mistakes.

'Is she all right?' he asks.

'She's had some disturbing news which has caused a migraine, Eddie. She won't be coming out.'

'Waldo, would you like a drink?'

'There should be a bottle open. Would you make me something to eat?'

'What would you like?'

'There's salmon in the fridge. Make it with the asparagus that's left over. Put a little mayonnaise on the side, please.'

'Of course.'

'And a little mustard.'

He brings it over and puts it on my tray.

'Aren't you eating? Would you put a film on? How about *Caligula*? Is it true that he suffocated the emperor Tiberius with bed pillows?'

'Who knows?' Then he says, 'It's raining hard, but as Zee's not up to anything tonight, I might pop out for a drink.'

'An old friend?'

'Yes.'

'How old?'

'Sorry?'

'Anyone I know? Could you do something for me before you go?'

Technically, he's good. I want him to help me move

a file from the recording machine I use sometimes to my iPad, where I can edit it better. It's a record of Zee's orgasms, and her whisperings with Eddie. A soundman I used to work with came to the flat and kindly helped set up some microphones.

There is other material on my phone – little videos and photographs – which I can transfer myself and cut together. My fingers aren't fast, but my equipment has voice recognition. It's like shouting at your editor in the cutting room.

I have cut various conversations together to make a continuous narrative that works well. There's a part of the recording I particularly enjoy, which I have played several times, like a Beatles single. Eddie says, 'I'm paranoid. Everyone says. But I keep thinking he can hear us. What will we do when he finds out?'

'I think you know, Eddie. Until then we can enjoy ourselves. Anyhow, he's so full of himself he can't see further than his nosey nose,' she says. 'There is nothing he can do. I own half of everything. Soon, when everything is clear – as we discussed – all of everything. We'll get out of this depressing place. Where would you like to live?'

'This area's a bit down at heel for me, I have to say. Coming back here always feels slightly wretched.'

'I know what you mean – the Russians, Arabs and

those covered women. Even little girls. I would never do that in London or let my daughters do it.'

'We're like strangers in our own city.'

'I don't want you to be a stranger anywhere. I've been looking through estate agents' material to find us a suitable place – with a wood-panelled study where I can lie on a chaise longue and watch you write your book.'

'And rooms for my children to stay? You haven't met them yet.'

'Oh, Eddie—'

'Yes, darling?'

'I'm not good with that kind of thing.'

'What kind of thing? I know we can become one family, Zee. My kids and yours. I can assure you, you will adore my kids—'

'At least the ones who aren't locked up.'

He says, 'I want to invite my daughter here next week.'

'Please, Eddie.'

'Zee, she has been pouring boiling water over her arms and the school claims she is uncontrollable. She needs to be supported. She can use the study here. It'll be a quiet place for her. You have daughters, you know how one can be beside oneself. We need to seek help for the girl.'

'Do that, Eddie—'

'My angel adores Anita's films. Do you think Anita would pop by here to meet my daughter? She gave me her phone number. I could text her this evening.'

'Text her? Eddie, I beg you, what are you talking about?'

'Don't you see, Francesca's had a hard time with me. She feels I let her down. Anita could be her mentor.'

'Leave her out of this. Waldo would hate that. He doesn't like Anita being used. As for your daughter, if she came, the other kids might follow. Where would it end? We could be overrun and I'd be hidden in my room. Waldo wouldn't put up with it. He's very protect-ive of me.'

Eddie watches me as I play this back through my Bose sound-cancelling headphones. What does a film director do? We lure audiences into a trap of pleasure by let-ting them watch crimes. Crime and love are the only subjects. We provide passion and cruelty. In return the public give us money and fame. It's honest work. It's witchcraft.

I nod at Eddie. 'Good man. The quality is fine.'

'What is the material you're playing with?'

'Sorry?'

'I thought I heard my voice. Wasn't that an image of me?'

'It was. You're more of a character than I am. I am

working on something which will interest you. A new form of movie. An "eargasm". It'll be called *Heaven's Gate.*'

'Wake up, Waldo, hasn't that title been used before?'

I hold up the evil eye of my phone and press the video recorder.

'Let me change it to *One Thousand and One Secrets*, then.' He's becoming impatient but cannot walk out. 'Do you still see Patricia? Pat Howard. She was married to a friend. I heard you know her.'

'I see her occasionally.'

'I'm going to invite her over for dinner next week. I want to freshen things up socially. I think she'll like Zee. Do you talk intimately with Patricia?'

He looks at the camera. 'Intimately?'

'Does she tell you who she loves? If she has a boy-friend?'

'Why would she?'

'Didn't you have her? There were rumours. I know you, Eddie. We've exchanged confidences in the past. And Zee and I talk. She adores my voice. She says I could have had a career on the radio, like Bob Dylan.'

'There are rumours about you too, my friend.'

'I hope they're libellous.'

'Weren't you with Anita?'

'Ah.'

'I've heard it said.'

'She's too beautiful for me, Eddie. Don't you believe me?'

'Many don't, Waldo. People say it's still going on. Zee has her suspicions. Actresses rely on directors.'

As he smiles and turns away, I say, 'You're cultured, Eddie. Were your parents knowledgeable? Is that where your curiosity comes from?'

Eddie snorts. 'My parents were ignorant in the way only English upper-middle-class Tories can be, Waldo. Stupidity, narcissism, and hedonism.'

'You're educated.'

'At boarding school I had a teacher . . . He gave me the depraved, contraband stuff. Dostoevsky, Baudelaire, Henry Miller, Godard, Billie Holiday . . . wine, even—'

'I know you like to be protected by an older man. What was his name? Didn't you write about him? *The Teacher Who Made Me.* Wasn't that it? What did he make you?'

He looks at his watch. 'Please, Waldo, I'd better move.'

'There's a crisp twenty on the table.'

He glances at it. His hand covers it. He picks it up. 'Kind of you, Waldo.'

'What was the teacher's name?'

'Bow.'

'You still see him?'

'He's dead.'

'How did he die?' He shakes his head. 'Smile at the camera.'

'Why are you doing this?'

'You make me creative again. It's terrible to have to retire. This is how Pelé must feel.'

'Waldo,' he says, 'I'm worried about Zee. Are you sure she'll be okay? Should we call a doctor?'

'I'll see how she goes tonight.'

'What has made her like this? Did she have something on her mind?'

'Like what?'

'I don't know—'

'Can I be honest with you, Eddie? It is true. We have been discussing you. You cause us to worry, and we consider ourselves to be like parents to you. I didn't want to excite you, but I've been making enquiries. I've taken things in hand. I'm pushing my contacts. I'm going to get you a professorship. I always say there are few people who talk about film as well or as often as you.'

'Waldo, thank you so much.'

'I'm grateful that you look after Zee for me, Eddie. You really are a good friend. There's no one like you in our lives.'

'Honestly, it's nothing.'

'If you have time, please call in tomorrow briefly to

pick up your things. Late in the afternoon. Very late, and bring oranges for the machine and some of that bread I adore, the ciabatta. If you have time, can you pop into the Algerian Coffee Store on Old Compton Street and get my usual dynamite? You've got the money now.'

'Okay.'

'Meanwhile, give me time to get her better. Don't worry, I'll take care of her. We'll be together all night.'

'You will?'

'Our marriage is the thing I'm most proud of.' I offer him my fist. 'One love, Eddie.'

'One love, Waldo.'

As I whistle 'Tomorrow Belongs to Me', he puts his washbag in his satchel and scurries out into the night. He has got the message and has gone for good. Or so I believe.

FOURTEEN

We are enjoying brunch. At least, she is. Scrambled eggs with smoked salmon. Toast on the side; coffee, fresh orange juice, melon with powdered ginger.

It cheers me up to watch her eat. She was one of the thinnest women in our circle, existing on dates – maybe one, or sometimes two a day – and yogurt and semen. Some women envied her, a good sign. But her weight worried me.

I am hungry and she knows it. A woman wants to give to a man, I've noticed. But only one man at a time.

'Don't you touch that toast, you bad, cruel thing. I bet you're hungry. Maybe you can have an almond biscuit later. Are you sorry now?'

'Don't be sadistic, Zee. You've become nasty.'

'So have you. He was humiliated. That was the least of it. I shudder at the thought.'

She is punishing me for pushing Eddie out into the dirty, unforgiving city. Apparently he walked; sat down; stumbled and staggered. He saw the sights, illuminated. All-night workers; early-morning workers; sex workers, thieves, the demented gesticulating. He phoned friends but they were indisposed. It was short notice. He dozed on a bench. You guessed it: he lost his wallet.

He's on his way here like a starved dog, yellow-faced, walking, if not hobbling.

'If you make me some eggs I'll tell you something important.'

She shows me the back of her hand. 'You've gone too far and I will have to take action. Were you delirious? You promised to find him work, and then you told him to call me mother.' She makes the eggs. She strokes my hair and removes my dribble. 'So, what is it?' I eat most of my eggs while she waits. 'Don't do this. Tell me.'

'Follow my instructions. Go to the window.' She does so. I'm behind her. 'See, there's a man waiting. Watching us. He's looking for Eddie. You get rid of one parasite and in no time there's another one biting you.'

'How long's he been there?'

'An hour or so.'

I pass her the binoculars. In his early fifties, with a shaved head, black-rimmed glasses and a cheap suit, he's about as wide as he is tall.

'Pure malevolence.'

She studies him. 'How do you know he's looking for Eddie?'

'I don't.'

'You could be right, for once.' She says, 'I'm going outside to confront him. I might slam him one.'

'Your recklessness is exciting. Don't do it, though.'

'He could hurt Eddie.'

'He won't. Not on the street. Does Eddie owe money?'

'So what? It's not a crime. Who doesn't owe money?'

'I don't.'

'We can help him out as we would with any friend. The man will go away.'

We are still together at the window. I hold her arm.

'He's coming,' she says. 'It's Eddie, turning the corner. The other man sees him. Eddie's smiling but he's nervous. I've never seen him like this. He's backing off . . .'

'It's too late. He's got him.'

'What should we do?'

The man approaches Eddie.

I say to Zee, 'Thank Christ Eddie's got my ciabatta.'

The man talks to Eddie. Eddie nods and glances up towards us. They're not unfriendly. Unfortunately the man doesn't touch Eddie, apart from laying his hand on his shoulder.

'He's only doing his job. He must be collecting money. He hasn't threatened him. But they know where he is. We must jettison Eddie, Zee.'

'As long as he's with us, he's safe. They won't touch us.'

117

'Bad people are looking for him. Bailiffs. Landlords. Probably the police. He could be a criminal. He's making us vulnerable.'

'I got your loaf,' he says a few minutes later.

'How did you get in?'

'Easy.' He holds up a key and smiles.

'How did you get it?'

'From Zee, to save you from inconvenience.'

'And the coffee?'

'No, Waldo. Sorry. I got into a spot of bother,' says Eddie. 'I forgot about the coffee.'

'Run into anyone you know?'

'No, no.'

He smells sour. He's dishevelled. I hope he doesn't fart on our new sofa; it's John Lewis, with a Biba blanket.

'What sort of trouble?' I say.

'What d'you think?' says Zee. 'A bit of money. Is it only money, Eddie?'

He nods. 'Greed.'

She says, 'Why do people make such a thing about a few pounds? Capitalism uses people and spits them out.'

'I beg your pardon?'

'I say what I like. It's free speech in this apartment.'

'Since when did you become a Marxist, Zee?'

'There's a lot you don't know about me.'

Eddie says, 'Only well-off, secure people can attack

others for their so-called materialism. It's a confident position of privilege to speak from. For the rest of us, there's a living to be made. I have to say it's quite a sickening hypocrisy.'

'It certainly is.' She says, 'Sit down, Eddie. Rest. Let me get you a blanket and a soft pillow. You must be broken.'

He slips his shoes off and lies back. We got the cushions in The Conran Shop. We paid too much for them, as you do there. But I like anything in faux fur.

I ask, 'How much do you owe?'

'Forty or so.'

'Grand?'

'Yes.'

'Christ.'

'And school fees. Other things. Feel-good merchants: doctors, psychiatrists, therapists . . .'

'Who was that man?' I ask him. 'The one outside.'

He holds his head. 'It's nothing. But Waldo, I didn't sleep. I'm broken. I can't continue like this—'

'Eddie, have you met him before? What's his name?'

Zee says, 'Since when did you become Maigret, Waldo? Eddie, take a bath and relax. Everyone's too excited right now. Waldo, it's time for your rest. Come on, old tortoise, let's get you out of harm's way.'

Out of harm's way? On my way to bed I go to the

window. The stocky guy looks up at me. He takes a photograph. I ride out onto the balcony, rise up as much as I can, and give him the finger. I take a photograph. He walks away.

Zee pushes me into my bedroom and helps me lie down.

I like the dark and quiet. It's a good opportunity for me to speak my diary. I've got plenty to say.

FIFTEEN

I work in my study, looking at the pictures and material I shot, attempting to bang it together as incoherently as possible, experimenting with music.

Eddie's stuff surrounds me: his newspapers, books. The photograph of his daughter which Anita dropped stares at me.

Behind me, he slumbers on the sofa through the morning. He wakes up when she takes him his coffee. They're in a hurry to go out. Since she helps him put a tie on, I guess they're going to the bank. Soon the lowlife's pockets will bulge, along with the wand in the front of his trousers.

They're starting a website featuring interviews with famous people. Eddie will use his contacts. Zee will squeeze me for mine; she's been attentive. They want to start with Anita, who is a keen talker but has never done her childhood: it would be a coup. Who wants the artist's work, when they can have it explained and stripped of the complication of artifice?

Zee leaves with Eddie. I zip onto the balcony and

watch them come out of the building. They approach the guy standing across the road. He's back there.

She was always tough and determined, Zee. When I was leaving India I was in a self-destructive phase. Alone and depressed, I'd considered retirement and suicide. Otherwise my philosophy was affirmative. Act – make an event. Smash the coordinates and see where the smithereens fly. Let in the madness, and be sure to be a danger to oneself and others. Too much thinking turns you into that fool Hamlet.

Or into Zee's husband, an affable, sweet-natured doctor who'd advised on the film. She and I were lovers by then. She'd driven me through Mumbai at night to my hotel. She'd shown me her earrings and told me she'd worn them for me. She asked to come to my room. She told me without equivocation that I smelled of loneliness. I wanted to argue with her. But she was right.

Not long after, I said, 'Zeena, I'm done here. Come with me. Bring the kids. Otherwise it's over and we'll both regret it. This might be a mistake worth making.'

She was about to move to Islamabad – the world's dullest town – with a husband who was devoted to his mother. She told me how she dreaded it. The mother-in-law was a strain and harassed her constantly. But she wanted to look after her. I asked why and she told me. I blanched but it didn't put me off her. I saw her differently. Zee's father was in an asylum, having strangled *his* mother to death, an understandable temptation which most of us resist.

Insanity isn't hereditary. Otherwise who would be untouched? Take me, I offer, a man who looks reality right down the line, one who knows we suffer more by trying to avoid suffering.

I packed up and headed to the airport. There she was, hand in hand with her two sweet daughters. She walked to me and never looked back. I will admire her for that forever. Her terror was that they'd end up like English girls, drunken, shameless, vulgar, underdressed. I assured her they'd inherit our respectability. The older one is visiting soon, sightseeing in London with her two kids. That will be a pleasure for Zee and should distract her.

I whirl to the window to see them leave the block. I get a close gander of them talking to the man. I learn nothing. The man walks off, to his car.

I watch a movie and text my movie star. I send her some photographs of the neighbours in their kitchens. To my surprise, Anita is not busy. She says she's on her way. She has to tell me something right away. I hope it's juicy. I'm impatient.

When she arrives I'm in my study, whizzing about like Ironside on acid, moving Eddie's stuff.

'Help me, baby. This is difficult for me.'

'I've been worrying. I'm glad to see you active. What are you doing?'

'I'm having a positive day.' I tell her, 'Please open the window.'

'You need air, Waldo? I thought a draught for you is like an amputation. What's going on?'

'We're going to fling Eddie's stuff out. It's started to sicken me. I've been weak. Help me, this is my last gasp.'

'What should I do?'

'Don't you do boxing now? Toss his gear through the window, baby.'

'Are you sure?' She says, 'Waldo, Zee will hate you for this.'

'She'll thank me in the very long run.'

Anita is reluctant but persuadable. We stuff his belongings in boxes and put my things back. I point to a large framed poster advertising a lecture of mine.

'I want this photograph of myself up there, Anita, please. I'm using Mao as my inspiration. "Cast away illusions. Prepare for struggle." I'm back in business, baby. You don't know you're stuck until you get moving.'

'Wise.'

'Hang it right there, please. I need to be centre-stage.'

We dust it, she knocks in the pins. I help her hold it up.

124

'A sinister guy has been watching us, Anita.'

'I know.'

'You know? How?'

'Waldo, listen. I'm at home last night, learning my lines. I get a text from him – Eddie. He's not with Zee, he says. She's not well and she's gone to bed. So he's at a club looking for company. The Six. He says, "Come by for a drink." I'm alone in my room and don't feel right.

'The evenings get oppressive. I know you say God made fags for women like me. After a certain age there aren't many people you want to listen to.'

'What do you want?'

'Someone I can say anything to. I read, smoke a joint, stretch, meditate – and then it's too much. I got in a cab and went to the Six. Do you mind?'

'I don't know yet.'

'I find Eddie there. Maybe I can investigate.

'It's a cramped, low-ceilinged basement with some chairs and tables, a small stage and a kitchen. Eddie has his oversized white jacket on. Look . . .'

There he is, on her phone, ungainly but sincere with his hair slicked back.

'He does three tunes including this one – "Come Rain or Come Shine". It isn't so awful. It's kind of heartbreaking . . . When he finishes he goes behind the bar and serves the customers.

'I'm sitting with a guy at his table. Gibney. The fellow who owns the club and runs other bars and restaurants. Even with me, Gibbo's one of those busy-everywhere people, always looking over your shoulder for someone who could be of more use.

'It turns out that that girl there,' – she shows me a photograph – 'it's Francesca, Eddie's daughter. You see, she's hiding behind her hair, but she's tattooed and pierced and the rest, as you see, witnessing this sad spectacle of her father.'

I notice she has a bandage on her lower arm, near the wrist. I guess she's the reason Zee didn't want to go to the club, if indeed she was invited. Behind the scarred daughter I glimpse the man Anita now describes – Gibbo.

'Gibney is a long-term Soho pal of Eddie's. They've known one another for years. Eddie helped Gibney at the beginning. When the place opened he invited all his well-known pals and word got round. Eddie even cooks there.

'I learn, mostly from the girl, that Eddie never tires of involving Gibney in his misfortunes. But, as with everyone he makes contact with, Eddie has strained his friend's patience.

'Gibney paid for doctors for the kids, helped out with the wives, placating and phoning with excuses and the rest. Often he lets the money go. Sometimes he doesn't.

'Gibney heard that Eddie was embarrassed and flung

out by you. Eddie's foothold at your place isn't as strong as Gibbo thought.'

'Shame.'

'He's been on at Eddie to get himself together. Eddie's despair and hopelessness have been worrying him a lot recently . . . The daughter, Francesca, is in a bad way. She phones Gibbo and weeps. He's no intellectual, Gibney.'

'A mercy.'

'He's an old-time Chelsea tough guy in his mid-fifties. Not one of those modern men with perfume and plastic muscles.'

'I'm thinking Tony Curtis in *The Sweet Smell of Success.*'

'Do.' She's finished with the packing. 'I went to some trouble for you. I've put some of the pieces of this puzzle together.'

We move to the kitchen table. She opens a bottle.

'Gibney is guiding Eddie; that's why he's been giving you the eyeball.'

'Ah.'

'He has a plan. He knows Eddie has nowhere to go and is edging towards the criminal. A year ago Eddie was desperate to pay his rent and forged a signature on a cheque. He just about got away with it after he confessed to Gibney, who paid the fellow back with his own money. He wanted to save Eddie from jail—'

'Why?'

'They're friends.' She shrugs. 'Eddie told Gibney he was thinking of becoming a life coach.'

'No better profession for a psychotic forger.'

'But Gibney conceived the excellent idea that as Eddie is good with the ladies—'

'Please, darling, I've witnessed him at work. His semen glistens on my best rug, if not on my wife.'

'Eddie has got to find a vulnerable rich woman, of which there are many in London.

'Eddie should hook up with one of these losers, settle down and collaborate with Gibney. Eddie can support his family and share the largesse—'

'Largesse, you say?'

'Houses, of course. Land. Paintings. Pensions and so on – with his old pal, his manager and sponsor, Gibney.'

'And who is the mark here?'

'Eddie has shown him photographs of this flat. They'll sell your home in the country, this place and your archive. Eddie and Zee will get a new apartment, and there'll be something left over for the business and the investments Gibney and Eddie have in mind once some money is freed up.'

'So we offer my life in order for Fast Eddie to spend the rest of his up to his ass in gold bullion? Perfect. They just have to wait for me to die.'

'You're an optimist.'

'I understand now. Why would they not want to speed it along? I am infernally alive, despite Eddie's efforts.'

'He resembles you. Eddie. Have you noticed?'

'Me?'

'You, as you were. As you are still, sometimes. Evasive, tricky. It's like you're being haunted by yourself.'

Thankfully we are disturbed. Zee has come home.

She's in a hurry and strides right over, standing with her hands reversed on her hips, taking in the boxes and looking at the photograph of Chairman Mao.

'I'm working in here on a new idea, Zee—'

'Waldo, explain to me, please. Is that Eddie's stuff you've packed? Anita, are you helping?'

'I can explain,' Anita says, as people do when they can't.

I say, 'It's ready for Eddie to take with him. He must have found somewhere by now. You remember, I didn't loan him the dough – I gave it to him in deep fondness. He's set.'

'He's our guest. He can stay until he's ready. Can't I invite my friends here?'

'He's been offered a job, thanks to me.'

'Yes, thanks, in Trivandrum, India, teaching the films of Clint Eastwood.'

'Finest work on God's earth, Zee. If the young are not educated, where would we be?'

She is looking at Anita. 'Have you touched Eddie's things again? Who gave you permission to behave like this in my apartment? Would I do this in your home? You think you're so famous you can do whatever you like?'

Anita's mouth moves about until she says, 'I'm sorry, Zee. But Waldo is being made anxious. We should be concerned about him. He's frail—'

'You're a despicable woman, whispering with my husband about me behind my back.'

I say, 'You're being vile, Zee.'

'Wait till I slap her.'

'She'll slap you.'

'Let her try.' Zee makes a cross on her cheek. 'How about right here?'

Anita sits down and stares at Zee, who says, 'Anita, unpack these things. If Eddie goes, I go.'

I say, 'Don't be ridiculous, Zee . . .'

To me Zee says, 'And you trust Anita? She is dating Eddie's pal, Gibney. They were drinking tequila and dancing. She taught him the Funky Chicken. She sang a song. She's come straight from him. He had her and took her out for breakfast. Eddie says she ate twice. Surely, Waldo, she must have mentioned it.'

'Is it true, Anita?'

'Dating doesn't describe it,' says Anita.

Zee pulls her rings from her fingers, and her earrings from her ears, before flinging them at me. She stamps off to her room. She throws a suitcase out into the hall and begins to put her things in it. I turn away.

I notice that Anita has closed her eyes and is practising a form of Tibetan breath control, designed, I presume, specifically for moments like this.

Her eyes open. 'Would you forgive her? Would you take her back?'

'Of course.'

'Why would you do that?'

'I was a man once, too. I'm familiar with bad behaviour and infidelity. I regret it, and would beg to be forgiven, if it were possible. Who hasn't had infatuations?'

'They want to rob you. Or worse.'

I shrug. Anita goes over to check on Zee.

She comes back. 'She says you're a bastard and she's leaving. She can't tell you where, and she will not be back. What should I say to her?'

'You're an actress: say goodbye to her for me in your nicest voice.'

'You can't stay here alone. Shall I get the nurse?'

'Why would I be alone for long?'

'What?'

'I'd be happy to cut my own throat.'

'Don't scare me.'

'Why would I want to carry on living alone and un-
loved?'

'The rest of us manage it.'

'Not me, baby. There'll be a martyrdom operation.'

'Jesus, Waldo, why do you have to be so extreme?'

The front door bangs and I hear the lift. I have no
intention of wheeling to the window to watch a woman
walk away.

Anita runs to the door; she is in the lift and soon, I
guess, she is outside, in the street. I wait, staring at the
wall.

She is away for a while: at least half an hour. I believe
I can hear raised voices but I could never be sure from
this distance. She returns out of breath.

'There's a deal.'

'Where's Zee?'

'There.'

And she is standing there, vibrating with fury.

She breaks my heart, that woman.

SIXTEEN

Something is occurring. For the next two days, Zee and Eddie come and go from the apartment. They are busily absent for hours.

I am not thrilled with Anita's 'deal': Zee will remain at home if she can invite friends to stay without my 'interference'. This 'friend' turns out to be Eddie.

He is cheerful, with an exciting future, and goes about his daily life as if he is at home.

Will Zee introduce Eddie to her daughter Samreen? I have assumed the flower of evil will disappear at least for the duration of Samreen's vacation. Samreen has taste and intelligence. Surely she won't like him? But now I can't be sure. Everything is tilting. I could be done for. I could be the one to recede. Zee has already asked me if I might be 'more comfortable' somewhere else. In my grave, I tell her.

On the third day, alone together, she makes a move. She proposes something.

'Shall we spend the evening talking and hanging around?' She kisses me. 'I'm sorry I've been so busy.'

She begins cooking early, around five. We open a good wine and chat in the kitchen. 'Tonight it is only us,' she says.

Since Samreen is arriving in a week we must discuss her itinerary. I explain how keen I am to accompany my adored stepdaughter to the theatre and to the tennis. I will be happy just to stroll and chat with her.

Before I make the perfect mistake, Zee and I talk about what we want to watch, and sit through a sizzling Joan Crawford. There are few sane characters in good movies. Hollywood was once the cinema of madwomen. Monstrous unleashed crazies with exceptional eyebrows and a knife or gun relax us both.

'These women know what they want,' I say.

'They're pitiless.'

Then, since I follow alternately the misfortunes of Manchester United and of each spousal debit on my iPad, I ask Zee if she could keep a tighter hold on her spending. I inform her that she has become extravagant. It must stop; we could be in danger. I am not earning anything. It's a race to see if I go bust before I die.

'The bank has warned me. I am closing the account tonight, Zee. The money will be controlled solely by me. You have some dough of your own.'

She gets up, her face flushed, and plumps the cushions

134

on the sofa. I become nervous, like a beaten dog whose cruel master raises a stick. But if a woman cannot pat cushions in her own home, what can she do?

She controls herself. Despite an upsurge of fury and flashing eyes, she helps me to bed and sits beside me, caressing my arm and hands. She pulls down the top of her dress to show me her breasts, letting me take her nipples into my mouth.

I thank her. 'Can I see your pussy?'

'Now?'

'I suspect it'll be the last time. I will consider it to be a reunion as well as an adieu.'

To my surprise she agrees. As she removes her underwear, I whisper, 'Oh, Zee, I regret already—'

'What is it?'

'That I will not live to see you as an old woman, at seventy, eighty, or ninety years old. I would kiss you even then. I hope you live a long time, and take care of yourself, my love. When I am gone, my love will follow you, and you will know that. My voice will guide you, if you want to hear it.'

Legs apart, she is sitting in a chair across from the bed. She is silent until she says, 'That's kind, Waldo.'

'Please stay in and watch over me. I am nervous tonight, Zee.'

She dresses, neither assenting nor disagreeing. I

relax and fall into a doze. It is early, and I wonder if Zee crushed a pill into my food.

I may be a foolish, drunken and otherwise idiotic old man, but I am aware when the front door bangs later that she has been getting ready in the bathroom. She has gone out for the evening. The poison of her perfume hangs in the air.

With the fury I have left, I drag myself out of bed and manoeuvre myself into my chair. My arms are starting to weaken, but I have always been determined. I locate some strength and scoot about headlessly.

It takes some time, and one of my hands has to hold the other, but I text Anita.

I wait impatiently. She replies fifteen minutes later, asking if I've fallen over. Am I sick? Should she send an ambulance? It is not that, I explain. I am in mortal danger. They are plotting.

She replies that she is thinking of me as she often does. I must rest this evening and look after myself. I am not losing my mind. And why would I be in any danger?

She is out tonight. She will pass by the flat tomorrow.

It could be too late. I stare at myself in the mirror. My face seems to have collapsed. My mouth hangs open, my lips tremble, as if I don't know what to say. My eyes stare in fright.

This hurts, especially at my age. I have been more

humiliated than I can bear. He haunts my dreams now.

I ask her to send me some comfort.

A few minutes later she sends me a selfie from a restaurant bathroom. It is a tight shot of her lifting her hair. She knows I appreciate her neck. I reassure her: she is looking good.

She sends another, wider shot.

At the edge of the mirror I recognise something. Or, rather, someone, walking past the open door. This is an opening I can use.

I call the owner. The world bursts into my ear.

'How are they?'

'Maestro, how good to hear from you! Where are you?'

'In purgatory.'

'I hope not.'

'On the other side – of the junction.'

'What a shame you are too poorly to be here,' Carlo informs me. 'I can see your dear friends enjoying themselves from my little window. My best waiter, Pietro, is looking after them. He can't hold his pad, it is twitching. He worships Anita and she is looking particularly beautiful in her leather jacket, black stockings and heels.'

'Bling?'

'Chains of pearls hang over her magnificent breasts. Maestro, can Pietro ask her for an autograph?'

'Of course not, Carlo. I'd be very offended. I'll send a

signed DVD tomorrow of *The Wrong Blonde*. Tell me: did they have the special?'

'The special "special" today is a beautiful creamy mozzarella which you would love, with some little tomatoes, basil and some oil. You would describe it as "juicy". Do you know the English call some mozzarella "buffalo" – as if it comes from the beast?'

'They do?'

'But only Mr Gibney asked for it.'

'What a man of taste Mr Gibney is. Do you know him?'

'Not at all.'

'What did Anita have?'

'The calamari.'

'A good choice. And the others? How are they?'

'Anita is pleased with the beautiful flowers Zee brought her. Did they perhaps have a disagreement?'

'Why do you say that?'

'There seems to have been some kissy-kissy making up. Now they are best friends, Maestro.'

'Phew. Is Zee eating well? You know how I worry. Or did she just have the fried zucchini and aubergine and leave most of it?'

'She started with that. Then she will smoke a cigarette and decide more.'

'Of course.'

The group is at a table by the window and they're on their mains. Carlo is specific when it comes to food. Gibney is enjoying steak and Eddie is having the sea bass.

'Does Eddie seem hungry?'

'He always eats enthusiastically while talking a lot, sir. But something has happened.'

'Sorry?'

'He has stepped outside. He paces up and down on his feet.'

'On the phone?'

'He seems to be worrying.'

'Is he alone? Has Mr Gibney joined him? Or perhaps Anita?'

'No, not Anita. She stays inside. She is very fascinated by Mr Gibney.'

'In what way?'

'Romantically. As if they are in one envelope. How she looks at him. Her lips are—'

'Where?'

'So close to his ear, Maestro.'

'Shocking.'

'Are they engaged, perhaps?'

'It's a matter of time.'

'I am pleased for her. How could such a woman go so long without a husband? We will have the reception here. You know we have a private room where we had the party for your prize.' There is a pause. 'Maestro, Mr Eddie seems upset about something and Zee is discussing it with him.'

'He does? Can you look into it, Carlo?'

'With respect, Maestro, how can I hear the details from here?'

'Send Pietro over. Put him nearby. He is our CCTV.'

'Certainly, Maestro.'

'Ask him to call Mr Eddie close and whisper something to him. Do not mention me. It's a lovely surprise which will cheer him up. But he must not let anyone else hear. You know how I like to be incognito. It's "Dear Pussy".'

'"Dear Pussy"?'

'"Dear Pussy".'

'I will write it down.'

'Don't. You will remember. "Dear Pussy". Whisper this password to me, Carlo, I beg you. In the voice of Silvio Berlusconi.'

'Sir, he is a waiter, not yet a comedian. But nonetheless . . .'

Carlo repeats it before the phone goes dead for a while. I hear voices in the background. Perhaps they are rehearsing. I wait.

Carlo comes back on the line. 'Are you there, Maestro?'

'How did he react?'

'With respect, not as well as you predicted, Maestro.'

'In what way?'

'He looked as though he'd swallowed a little pin. He stared around the street wildly for the person who put it in him. Up and down, here and there, round and about as if for an assassin with a gun. He smacked his fist against his forehead.'

'Did he go and sit down again?'

'Zee comforts him. She thinks he is dizzy from the alcohol.'

'Please, Carlo, be sure to get a photograph of the whole table in their delirium. Send it to me so I can revel in my friends' enjoyment.'

'That will be difficult. But for you I will do it, Maestro.'

'As I said, don't mention me, Carlo. If they knew how I writhe here with worry it would interfere with their pleasure.'

'Of course, Maestro. I know how you think of others.'

A few minutes later a photograph of them all at dinner pings into my phone. Sam Spade couldn't have done it better.

I am cheerful and laugh so much I defecate in the bed. The shit keeps coming, more and more of it, rising up around me like a remorseless tide, until it reaches the ceiling and I lie drowned in a sarcophagus of faeces.

SEVENTEEN

The sound of heavy rain, and a noise which makes me open my eyes. Drifting cigarette smoke. A sidelight switched on.

It is night. I come round and sit up a little. From my mirror I can see into the mirror in the living room, where she stands in a tight, ankle-length, sheath-like dress, smoking.

I can't see Eddie but I can, I believe, hear him. I make an effort to move position until I catch the top of his head. His face is in her thighs. He is drooling into her legs, snatching at her dress.

'What are you doing down there, Eddie?'

'You are horny and I apologise. I wish I could satisfy you tonight. I can try and give you some pleasure.'

'I'm unattractive now?'

'I'm disturbed.'

'Why would you be, when everything is going well, and we have talked through our future? But it happens sometimes.' She lifts her head a little and for a moment seems to be looking straight at me. 'Though rarely to

Waldo. He is very sensual. He had an eager penis all his life.'

'I'm not a machine, Zee. This pace is impossible for me.'

She says, 'I'm an old woman but even tonight Waldo wanted to see my pussy.'

'You showed him?'

'He begged, Eddie. He is my husband.'

'That's no excuse. I can't believe it. Suppose I showed my cock to my wife. What would you say?'

'Would your wife want to see your cock?'

'Not necessarily.'

'It's too late. He's looked now.' He groans and she says nothing, until, 'Does Gibney have other women?'

'Why do you ask?'

'You sound uncertain, Eddie. Don't you boys discuss everything? Waldo will go crazy if he finds out. He's fond of Anita.'

'It's got nothing to do with Waldo.'

She asks, 'Is Gibney a liar? You know I don't like liars, Eddie. You've given all that up, haven't you? Despite everything, I like Anita. She tried to be kind.'

'She did?'

'She was wild when I tried to run away. She gave me what Waldo calls "a tremendous bollocking". She said I should do my duty, not follow rainbows, and be devoted

144

until he passes. After, I'd be free to do what I like with any conman I fancied—'

'She called me that?'

'She called *me* everything—'

'What did you say?'

'She knows I appreciate loyalty. It's the only value we have on the subcontinent. I just hope that uneducated crook doesn't mess her about.' I cannot hear his reply. Zee says, 'Get up, for God's sake, man. Where's my lighter? I can be a difficult woman. I'm not a filmi star, but at least I have two men devoted to me.'

I guess Eddie gets up off his knees. It takes some time. At last his head appears. 'You do? Who, apart from me?'

'Waldo, of course.'

'I've told you, he doesn't matter. Why do we have to have this discussion?'

'How could he not matter? He's creative, he's admired. I ask myself in the middle of the night: how did I do it? Capture the attention of one of the most fascinating men? There are books about him. There's a new one over there.'

'What does it say?'

'It's a piece by a friend who worked with him. It made me laugh. Waldo's rude, lazy, capricious, anarchic and a provocateur. Wherever he goes, he shakes things up.'

Eddie sounds weary. 'Does that mean a lot to you?'

'The places we go, the hotels, the dinners and friendship with famous people. It isn't because of me, dear. Do you really think anyone cares a damn what I think? Half the time they don't look at me or remember my name. You have to be careful with the English. They don't like show-offs. Waldo protected me.' She says, 'I will have to cross back into the ordinary world at some point.'

Eddie is disappointed. 'I can't give you what he can. That's what you're saying.'

'You get invited places, don't you? You're always scurrying here and there.'

'I go along to things, yes. I can find out where everything takes place. You'll come with me, won't you?'

'You make me sound like a pet.'

'So far you've been treated as a grand woman—'

'Because of him? Is that what you insist on saying?'

'You don't notice, but people genuflect,' he says. 'I'm afraid you'll miss it. I won't know to keep you entertained.'

'As long as we don't have to spend time with Gibney, we'll see.'

'No one has stood by me like him.'

'A man like you can do better than that spiv.' Then she sighs. 'Eddie, quiet. Don't just chatter on. Your noise is like a dagger in the head. What is that awful look on your face?'

'Not only have you been displaying your vagina, but I've been thrown into a mad mood, Zee. Look, I'm shaking. I heard something frightening. From the waiter at the restaurant.'

'Pietro?'

'He came over, smiling absurdly. And whispered, "Dear Pussy, Pussy, Pussy".'

There is a silence. I stuff the duvet into my mouth to stop myself laughing.

'I started feeling queer, Zee. I'm hearing things, as you said you do. Waiters don't just say "Dear Pussy" to customers at random. I've told no one the school story.'

'Not quite no one. Gibney and I are not no one.'

'Zee, darling, please, you wouldn't tell anyone, would you?'

'I'm trying to elevate you. Why would I inform a waiter that you were buggered by your music master as he whistled *Don Giovanni*?'

'Didn't you tell Waldo?'

I imagine her shaking her head and looking around as if for a handy exit.

At last, 'I mentioned it.'

'Did you tell him about the rest? How we went to the teacher and Gibney lost his temper and attacked him?'

'Some of it might have slipped out. Waldo is very persuasive, Eddie. He has a grip on me.'

'What a bastard he is, planting a wasp in my head.'

'That's why only you can help me escape. He's suffo-cating us. Let's get it over with and be free.'

'How can we be free when you've made such a lunacy with your talk?'

'Being raped is nothing to be ashamed of. These days people go on television to discuss it. We should put your account on the website, with a photo. You wrote about it once in a psychology magazine.'

'I refused to give my name.'

'You should now. It would create traffic. Waldo says it would make a solution out of a problem.'

'That's sick. I don't want to make a career as a rape victim. What would the children think? I'm disgusted to even think about it.'

'You weren't a victim. That's what's interesting. You couldn't wait to be raped. You wore tight trousers.'

'That is mad.'

'I like you when your blood is up.' There is a pause. 'Don't forget, you've killed before.'

'Who?'

'Bow.'

'But he jumped before he could go to jail.'

'With your encouragement, Eddie, let's face it. You helped him make the decision. It was a good job, well done. The best thing you did.'

148

'I didn't do it!'

'I've added it to your credit, darling.'

There is lots I can't hear. I sip my vodka and gargle with it. I enjoy imagining him with his head in his hands, wondering what he's got himself into.

'Don't blub or turn against me, Eddie, when I'm exhausted from trying to work things out. Remember, I'm the one keeping you from destitution. Didn't Gibbo say tonight that he couldn't see any way forward for you? Unless . . . ?'

'Unless . . . unless . . . What can I do, Zee? What do you want from me?'

'Without me, Waldo would put you out on the street. He's ruthless. Count your mercies.'

'I'm trying to do that.'

'You want us to have a future. You need to be manly. You know what the kiss-off is.' There's a pause. 'What is that noise? Is it Waldo? Will you see to him?'

'Why is it my turn?'

'You won't enjoy paying your own bills, and they're considerable . . .'

Eddie comes into my room, turns on a light and looks at me.

'Are you awake, dear friend?'

'Can you turn me over?'

As he is doing it, she comes in behind him.

'It's easy. Do this.' She snatches up a pillow. 'You are a nuisance, Waldo. You've been naughty, you know you have. I'm tired of your meddling. Let me see you.'

She holds the pillow over my face. She pushes down.

Eddie grabs her arm. 'Zee!' he says. 'He can't breathe!'

She stops. Eddie stares at her.

'God, Zee— We could go to prison for this.'

'Eddie, please, this is mercy. We'll ask for it one day. Do it in stages. Take your time. I can't tell you the number of times he's begged me to let him go. He's had enough. Let eternity take him and we can be free.'

At the door she stops.

'When you're done, Eddie, come into my arms. I'll be waiting.'

EIGHTEEN

She steps in, kisses him on the cheek and leaves.

He leaves me too. But I can hear him moving about in the living room. His hands are not still.

I am getting impatient. He must get on with it before I fall asleep. I don't want to miss anything. If you can't enjoy your own death, what can you enjoy?

'Eddie, Eddie . . .'

This brings him to the doorway. She has left the pillow on the end of the bed. He picks it up and moves towards me.

'Now I can see you. Pussy, Pussy, Pussy—'

'Those are disgusting and insulting words,' he says.

'Didn't you do unforgivable things behind my back? You took what's mine. How could you do that to a friend?'

Eddie says, 'Hit me, if you can. I'm weak. My body was never my own. I try to please everyone. I got used to servicing people, it's like a favour, you know it how it is . . .'

I crook my finger and bid him to come closer.

'Eddie, billions have committed murder, and lived with it too. I know that tonight you must do it. Walk into the light so I can see your murdering eyes.'

I think he's going to cry. He covers his face with a pillow. 'There is a smell in here,' he says.

'Eddie, I have no objection to being murdered. It'll add glamour to the last page of my CV. But do you have doubts? You should. She will imprison you. You love your life as it is.'

'Why would being with Zee be worse than the hell of insecurity I already live with?'

'You'll be trapped here in our life, not yours. And what you think you want you will never have, even if you have it. She likes bad boys, ones who take liberties, who care nothing for the consequences. While you are weak. She will enslave you. You won't have a moment's freedom.'

He stands there limply. Then he picks up his courage again and comes towards me.

'Are you going to do it now, Eddie?'

To cheer him up, I make a noise I want him to believe is my death rattle.

As he approaches, I push a button on my iPad and the TV turns on. The picture is big; the sound, from my monster subwoofers on two sides, is like an attack. We hear Johnny Rotten's voice: 'No future! No future!'

Music to die by.

'Look, Eddie, it's my new one,' I say. 'My new film. Will you watch a moment or are you in a hurry?'

Johnny's voice fades. A black screen. A voice, 'Hello, I am dead', is my announcement.

I'll record that again if I'm not dead tomorrow and have some spare time. It sounds a little hollow, hammy and Wellesian.

'This is me, Waldo, addressing you from beyond the grave. From hell, I hope. At least it's warm. And this is my final story. Here – this is Zee . . .'

There she is, fussing about.

'This is Eddie. Hear him . . .' A few chirrups and some shuffling from Eddie. 'And here I am . . .'

My voice, my beard – a big selfie and a wolfish smile.

I say, 'You can't deny anything, Eddie. There are many images. Look – here is your man Gibney outside my apartment. Here's Zee. You are at dinner. Carlo took a lovely picture of you all.'

There are photographs of Zee in many different positions. Soon there is her voice and the *Götterdämmerung*, her orgasms.

'Everything is recorded now, Eddie. Look up at the cameras and wave goodbye.'

'This is crazy, Waldo. I never intended to kill you. Where did you get that idea? I've only wanted you to be comfortable . . .'

He backs away.

'By the way,' I call after him. 'Ask your mentor Mr Gibbo to contact me. We must talk.'

I hurt in every part of myself. What an evil pain is. But I cannot even rest. I can hear them arguing in the living room. She cries, 'Eddie, you messed it up, as you do everything!'

There is heavy movement followed by a male cry. One of the mirrors is knocked over. She is chasing him, I suspect, as he tries to gather his things. She has caught him a blow. I hope it is on the head. He has grabbed her, I guess, and she could be strangling him, she is capable of it, his cries sounding fainter, her breathing louder. Although I'm keen for him to be dead, and would love to see his head on a plate, I don't want his body rotting on my living room floor, or my wife behind bars.

I gather my strength and slide out of bed to intervene. Before I reach my chair, I slip and fall. I am flapping on the floor, where I can only groan and attempt to cry out, like an elderly Gregor Samsa.

At last the door bangs. The darkness echoes.

Being almost murdered has exhausted me.

NINETEEN

Samreen says, 'What's happened, dear Waldo?'

I turn as much as I can. 'Tell me what you mean, sweet Sammy . . .'

Her black hair flows down over her trench coat. She wears a wool scarf even in this weather, as she pushes me through the city, leaning forward to reach my ear.

'Mum moves more slowly. That's natural as one ages. But she looks at you and she listens. She pays attention. This is new. When she walks in the park with the children, she lets them lead her. She was never like that with us.'

'How was she?'

'Frustrated and angry. She didn't want to be with us. You know she was, let's say, quite strong with her children?'

'I had some idea.'

'With my father too. She said, "He doesn't even beat me." When she'd been angry and hit us she was contented. Or she would hold us down in the bath until we thought we would drown. After waterboarding us, she'd eat well. But she knew she couldn't do the mad stuff with you.'

'Why not?'

'Waldo, you rescued her. Once she got you, she lost interest in us, thank God. But I was angry for years. After so long, I like her a bit more.'

'Me too.'

'Truthfully, has she ever been that way with you? You don't answer. She'd suffocate us, you know.'

'Yes.'

'And you? Again you don't reply, Waldo.' I turn to look at her, but she looks into the distance. 'I will speak to her in the next few days.'

'Why?'

'I'm afraid she'll die before we've talked it through and I'll be left with mouthfuls of unused words.'

'I hope you say it. I like a Hollywood ending.'

Zee is at the movies with the children. Samreen enjoys taking me round the old places: Earl's Court, South Kensington, Chelsea. It looks unrecognisable to both of us. We stop outside the Troubadour and talk. But not for long. Samreen doesn't know it, but I have to be somewhere. I text Anita and tell her to prepare. I am on my way. She knows what to do. I am not one for revenge, but in Gibbo's case I can make an exception.

'I have a new slowness too,' I tell Samreen. 'And I love Zee as much as ever.'

'She loves you. The way she looks at you. And she is a little afraid of you, as usual. There is a new melancholy there. What is that? Why did you ask me to come to London a few days earlier?'

'You must talk to Zee about that.'

'Don't blaspheme near her now, wise Waldo.' She goes on, 'Mama's hair is undyed and she sits with her Koran and prayer beads, counting. I see there is a prayer mat in her room. The Arabic words must calm her. Religion tells you everything when there is disarray. But yesterday, on the street, she was wearing a long skirt, and she covered her head.'

'Did you ask her why?'

'No. Even here, in London, people look at covered women with hatred. I wonder if she will fast? We did as children because of my father, but has she done it recently?'

'I wouldn't have it: she's thin as it is.'

Sammy says, 'Mummy was alienated from the truth, she says. There is materialism, mental disease and perversion. The hijab makes her feel strong. Did she fall under the influence of someone evil?'

'God is easily taken in, Samreen. He's asleep and he's a fool. As a devout sceptic, I am not so gullible. All

I can say is, I intend to go on with this marriage until I die.'

'Mine is coming to an end, Daddy. How did you keep yours alive so long?'

'Genius.'

She says, 'You know what my mother's greatest fear is? Of losing you. Of your death. It has haunted her. "Without him there'll be nothing," she says.'

She pushes me on, a long way, until we get to Carlo's. It is after lunch. There is a table by the window. We can have tea.

Zee replaced Eddie with God: a wise choice, in my view. But I do wonder what this disillusionment and the collapse of her hopes will do. She will recover, I believe. It will take time. Not that I have that.

'Waldo, wake up,' says Samreen. 'That man is waving at you. Over there, across the road, isn't that your friend?'

She turns me around. It is Anita, with Gibney. She has brought him along. I am pleased to see him. It is time for some shock and awe. Time to bite the head off the snake.

He is pleased too. He is trying to cross the road towards me, with some urgency.

'Are you sure you want to talk to that man, Waldo? He looks a little angry. Is he Anita's PR?'

Anita, behind him, comes over to kiss me as Gibney looks on, wondering how to approach this. For a moment he looks at a loss. Illness has some consolations: you can't grab a man in a wheelchair by the lapels and hurl him into the traffic.

Gibney offers his hand but I can't touch it. He bends forward to address me.

'Ah, Waldo, I've been trying to get hold of you. Would you join me a moment to discuss your unreasonableness?'

'There is no man keener to hear the truth about himself, Mr Gibney. I only hope you will take the time to show me your cosh.'

Samreen asks if I mind being left. She excuses herself to do a little shopping. She'll be back later to pick me up. Anita agrees to take over. They exchange phone numbers in case I have a queer turn.

I have my objections to Mr Gibney but there are things I want to know. Doesn't civilisation mean keeping your temper when there is no reason for restraint?

We sit down, Anita bearing the fearful look of a walnut about to be placed in a nutcracker. What can she do except pick at her fingers? Pietro fetches the menu; Carlo comes out and throws himself over us. I ask Pietro for my favourite lapsang and a jug of hot water.

At last I say, 'It is unusual not to see you lurking

159

outside my house like a man about to steal the pictures, Mr Gibney. Are you keen to see my Peter Blake or other possessions?'

'Not interested.'

'How is your boy Eddie?'

'You'll know something about it. He's been ill and injured on the shoulder and in the eye. He's in a hostel.'

'Grim?'

'The smell isn't gorgeous. He shares a room with six other men. And he's working in the bar at the club.'

'How are your new plans developing? Patricia Howard's the new mark, isn't she? She's coming to dinner. I'll be sure to discuss it with her.'

'Why would you object to people being introduced to one another?' says Gibney. 'Anita did mention that you were isolated and paranoid, with a filthy temper—'

'Gibbo,' Anita says. 'That's enough. He's not paranoid.'

Gibney takes her hand and pats it while he speaks to me. 'Eddie called you Master. He liked to spend time with you. He said you knew what you were doing.'

'That's a nice thing to say. Can I ask you something? Why did he have the bad taste to play with my wife? Or would he play with just anyone's wife? I've heard he was somewhat indiscriminating.'

Gibney snorts. 'I'm reluctant to be the one to inform

160

you, but your wife was gagging for it. You hadn't noticed? What were you looking at all day? He was satisfying her. I'm afraid it was a fitter man's work. She took him, and she did him over, promising to set him up in business and find him a flat and other stuff. She conned him, and, I'm afraid to have to tell you, he didn't find sex with her congenial.'

I glance at Anita. 'If you really are rough trade, Mr Gibney, I'm going to be very disappointed if you don't do something nasty today. I have some standards, and would never trust anyone who wears pointed shoes. But you are, I hear, Eddie's manager. Your slave didn't get the money or the woman, but you nearly took down a sick man with your scheme to enrich yourself through him.' I add, 'You are aware that your boy also tried to murder me?'

Gibney, who is a jumpy, nervous fellow and appears to be doing something irritating with his face, laughs at this.

'How can Eddie be the murdering sort? Your wife had a grudge against you. You two crooked darlings tried to pin the blame on him.' He leans towards me. 'Zee's aggressive and never described you as anything but a monster. I've been worried about Eddie and his devotion to you both. Your wife took him for a right ride with her wiles and words.'

'In what way?'

'You were happy to let him be used by your wife while he kept her satisfied. Nothing is for free, everyone pays for sex. She knew it would cost her now . . . But when he demanded some equality you tormented him, poor man. You messed with his head. You mocked his kids and the abuse he went through. You both knew what had happened to him in the past, didn't you?'

'I was made aware of the part you played in the demise of Bow.'

'That's also my fault, is it?'

'It lifts me to hear how blameless you are, Mr Gibney.'

He says, 'Eddie was found collapsed on the street when he finally escaped that night. She attacked him with a Golden Globe—'

'A Bafta. They're well made.'

'She hurt him badly because he didn't do what she said. He ran from you, out of London, towards the airport, where he intended to fly somewhere to escape for good. He had taken a substantial overdose and had to be carted off to hospital. His daughter has had a kind of breakdown. They both need a lot of care. I am very disappointed in your family, Waldo. And I'm letting you know that—' He takes Anita's hand, holds it up and kisses it. 'At least I have her.'

I've had enough. No more jouissance for you, mister.

I turn on my little camera and hold it up with one hand. I lean across the table and with one swipe of the other hand tip the jug of water into Gibbo's lap, over his thighs, one hand and crotch. I'm weak, but it's a good shot and perfectly aimed. The hot water does its work. I take a breath and watch him with pleasure. Up he leaps, crying out, wounded and mad. As he hops about, flapping at his genitalia, I reverse away from the table, keeping my camera on him. Posterity won't miss a moment.

I say to Anita, 'Now he'll think twice about getting in my way again.'

Before he can attack me, Anita holds down his arms and rushes him to the bathroom to pour cold water over his sizzling parts.

I can see Samreen hurrying back towards me as Carlo and Pietro gather round.

'What is it, Waldo?' she says. 'Have you finished your tea already?'

'Yes,' I say, in the uproar. 'And I did what I came for. It's been an excellent day. Sometimes it feels good to be alive.'

TWENTY

We have a party. The kids, Samreen, friends. Carlo and Pietro come across from the restaurant bringing cakes.

Anita takes my hand and tells me not to fret. With Gibbo it's dead and done for. Some foolishnesses are worth it. But this was fun that stopped being fun. She is not complaining. She has gained a friend: Francesca, Eddie's daughter.

'I'm taking her to a gallery and then to a movie. I can be of use in that way,' she goes on. 'She's a decent singer. She can play drums and piano . . .'

At the table, with the people I love around me, I am barely awake. There is a shadow over everything; the world has become silent, as they say it does before a tsunami. Laughter, chatter, clinking glasses and cutlery fade in and out. I am more than a little absent but I like to believe my face shows my relative content despite everything.

I have seen my death in their eyes. Dying certainly does for your looks. They are shocked by my appearance. Having shrunk into myself, I am gaunt; my eyes are too big for my face; my mouth twitches and people think I'll vomit on them.

Everyone is being so kind it is clear I am near the end. After so long, I am less impressed by death than I used to be. I am thinking of my early life: my mother and father, and I forgive them, as I hope to be forgiven myself. I think of the women I've loved, and those who loved me. I consider Zee, Samreen and Anita going through my things when I'm gone, sending my clothes to the charity shop, sifting through my papers, and photographs; I hope they look at the material I shot in the last few months. I wonder how long Zee will stay here without me, or whether she'll go to the US with Samreen.

'I need to lie down,' I say to Zee.

I am dust and my story ends here.

'I'll take you.'

The friends don't stay long. The children say goodnight and the women get me to bed.

Zee caresses my head the way I like it. She answers my questions, but for a while has been quiet, as if stunned. She wanted me gone. She will have her wish.

Old age is the new childhood: she strokes and kisses me, her husband and baby. She says my name. I drift away.

This is as decent a way to go as any. Everything has been said, except her name. 'Zee . . . Zee . . . You forgot about me for a time. But now you remember me. That's all I want. There was only ever you.'

The breath of her love on my face. Dying's not so bad. You should try it sometime.